the Fear Zone 2

the Fear Zone 2

K. R. Alexander

ISBN 978-1-338-70213-2

10 9 8 7 6 5 4 3 2 1   21 22 23 24 25

Printed in the U.S.A.   40
First printing 2021

Book design by Baily Crawford

To those who refuse to let their fears define them

April

We thought the nightmare was over.

Andres and Deshaun and Kyle and Caroline and me—two years ago, we faced our fears. We vanquished them. No more nightmares of snakes or sharks or being buried alive. No more ghosts haunting the hallways.

No more vengeful clowns.

For two years, we started to believe we could move on and leave all the scary stuff behind us. We let ourselves believe we were victorious.

We were wrong.

Now we're starting to learn the truth:

You can face your fears. You can overcome them. But then you grow older. You change.

And your fears grow and change too.

We should never have let ourselves believe we were safe.

Kyle

"Were we ever that tiny?" Andres asks as we pass by the elementary school.

I look over to the kids playing on the playground. Swinging and playing tag and laughing in the cool autumn afternoon. I watch as one of the girls jumps into an enormous pile of leaves, giggling as they cascade around her.

I suppress a shudder—the sound of rustling leaves sounds way too much like hissing for my liking.

"No," I say. "I'm pretty certain we skipped that age and became, like, old people overnight."

Andres's grin slips.

Neither of us mentions what happened two years

ago. Neither of us says *why* we had to grow up so fast. We don't have to. The memory is burned into both of us like scars.

"Why are we meeting them here, anyway?" I ask. "Isn't it a little strange that we're hanging out at the middle school?"

Andres shrugs and sits down on a bench, watching the kids play. "April said she wanted us to meet here," he says.

I sit down next to him, our shoulders almost brushing. I feel like I should say something.

I'd been joking about growing up overnight, but as we sit there, staring at the kids who don't seem to have a care in the world, it's clear the words couldn't have been more accurate, or more cutting. It's like we're a different species. Not just older, but more . . . I don't know, *aware*. We know that there are true evils out there. We know there are monsters that go bump in the night. To these kids, it's all just make-believe. To us, it's deadly real.

A wind rustles through the trees, scattering leaves across our feet. Hissing.

Lately, all I hear is hissing.

"Don't you two look cheerful," someone calls out.

I jolt and look behind me to see Deshaun, April, and Caroline walking our way. Deshaun and April are holding hands, and Caroline is leaping through the small piles of leaves lining the sidewalk.

April waves when we make eye contact, and Andres jumps off the bench to go give her a hug. I slide off and walk over, bumping fists with Deshaun and embracing the girls.

"Good to see you guys," April says. Even though we're all in the same high school now, we don't get to see each other very much during the school day. April and Caroline and Andres are sophomores, while Deshaun and I are juniors. With everyone in different school activities, well, it's hard to actually find time to meet as a group. I always see Andres because we're dating and Deshaun because we're still best friends and I live with his family now. But I don't see the girls as much.

"Yeah," I say. Another breeze blows past.

Hisses past.

I burrow deeper into my coat and try not to look bothered. *It's just the wind, Kyle. Just the stupid wind.*

"What did you want to meet us here for?" I ask. "Couldn't we have met somewhere a little warmer?

I don't know about you, but I could use some hot chocolate."

April rolls her eyes, but her expression goes serious immediately. She steps a little closer and lowers her voice.

"I just thought . . ." She takes a deep breath and looks around, as if trying to catch someone listening in. But the kids are all playing and completely ignoring the group of high schoolers huddled at the edge of the playground. "I thought it made sense for us to meet here. Because tomorrow is Halloween, and . . . tomorrow marks the day we all got the notes."

Chills slither down my spine at the thought. She's talking about the notes that dragged us to the graveyard. The notes that led us to unleash the clown and all its terrible nightmares.

I swear the air between us drops twenty degrees.

"C'mon, April," Andres says. "Why'd you have to bring that up?"

"Because it's important for us to remember." She glances around the group, but it's clear from everyone's expressions that we *do* remember. And we wish we could forget.

April goes on. "We've all been so busy—I haven't

seen all of you guys for weeks. And, I don't know, I thought we should get together. To sort of prove to ourselves what we did."

"We don't need to prove anything," Andres says. "It's over. Behind us. We need to move on. *You* need to move on."

I don't say anything. Because even though I agree, I also know that as April's best friend, Andres is able to say what the rest of us probably shouldn't. I can tell from her expression that she isn't letting this go. Deshaun squeezes her hand.

"I don't want to remember the bad stuff either," she continues. "That's not the point. I wanted us to celebrate coming together. I wanted to celebrate our friendship, because that's what defeated the evil in the first place."

Another breeze rustles around us, tumbling leaves over my sneakers. The noise almost drowns out April's words.

"I was thinking we could go to the carnival tomorrow," April says. "It's their opening night, and they're doing free entry for kids in costume. It would be a lot of fun."

I look over to a group of kids huddled on the

other side of the playground, just like us. It looks like they're passing homework or something around between them. One of the kids looks over—he has bright red hair and freckles, and when he sees me looking at him, he quickly looks away.

"That sounds great," Deshaun says. "Saves Kyle and me from candy duty."

"Then it's settled," April says. "Cancel your Thursday plans: Tomorrow night we go to the carnival."

"And I was talking to my dad," Caroline chips in. "I was thinking we could do a sleepover Friday night. Maybe watch some scary movies and eat left-over candy?"

We all voice our agreement. I don't think we've ever been to Caroline's house. Normally when we do sleepovers or game nights, it's at my place or April's. Not that those have happened much lately; we've all gotten so busy.

"I guess I should ask," Deshaun says timidly. "No one got any notes today, right?"

To our collective relief, everyone shakes their head.

"Good," he says. "It's still over."

Another gust. Another hiss. Another leaf sliding across my ankles.

I look down as my friends discuss the details
        and see a snake slithering over my shoes.
I yelp and jump back.
But the snake isn't there. It was never there.

"Are you okay?" Andres asks. He takes my hand and gives it a squeeze. I can't return the gesture. My heart hammers too loudly in my ears. My hands feel numb.

"Yeah," I lie. "I'm fine."

Deshaun

"Dude, you're not fine," I say.

We're sprawled out in my bedroom, Kyle on the floor and me on the bed. Even though he has his own room, he pretty much only uses it for sleeping. Otherwise, he hangs out in here with me. Just like old times.

Kyle pauses the game he was playing and looks up at me. I set down my homework and return the stare.

"What?" he asks.

"Earlier, on the playground. You looked like you saw a ghost."

"Snake," he corrects me before swallowing and looking away. "I thought I saw a snake."

That makes me pause. I shuffle closer to him and put a hand on his shoulder. He doesn't brush it off. I don't really know what to say.

Of all of us, Kyle still seems the most haunted. Maybe because his fears were rooted in reality; they had manifested long before we were given the creepy notes that dragged us into the graveyard. Even though we've been best friends since elementary school, he still won't really tell me what happened in the years before he moved in with us. I know enough. I know his dad was horrible to him, keeping snakes in the basement and threatening Kyle with them daily. I know that for Kyle the appearance of the clown hadn't been as scary as the real nightmare waiting for him at home.

I know because even though the clown is gone and our fears are no longer following us around, even though Kyle now lives with me, he still has nightmares. He still wakes up yelling out in fear. We share a wall. I've heard it more nights than I can count.

We defeated the clown. We faced our fears. We got Kyle out of his house. But for Kyle, the nightmare never really ended. It got buried deeper . . . but it's still there.

"Are you sure?" I ask.

He doesn't look at me when he nods.

Even though I want to convince myself that everything is behind us, I'm not like Caroline or Andres or April. I'm not willing to believe it's all over. It doesn't feel safe.

I haven't told anyone—not even Kyle—but every day, I expect the nightmare to start again. Every day, I wake up believing that the last two years were just a dream, and that reality is just waiting to smack us in the face. Every day I flinch at shadows or gusts of wind. I double-check to make sure that nothing in my room is out of place. I ensure the precautions I set up around my room are still intact: bowls of sea salt by the windows and doors. Quartz crystals under the mattress. Lit candles and incense to keep away bad energy. I've even hidden some charms in Kyle's room, just in case. Not that I expect them to work—they didn't before—but I have to at least try to do what I can.

It feels like all those preparations are about to be put to the test.

My chest constricts as we sit there, silent.

Maybe it was your imagination, I want to tell

him. *Maybe it was a twig. Maybe it was just a normal snake.*

But I don't say anything. Because I believe Kyle saw what he saw.

"Do you think it's coming back?" I ask. The words come out before I can stop them, the one question I don't want an answer for.

"I don't know," he says after a long pause. He sighs. "Maybe it was just my imagination. I didn't sleep much last night. Was cramming for the history exam."

I know it's a lie—his voice is too light, and he wouldn't have brought it up if he thought there was a chance he'd been imagining it. But I don't push it.

"You're not going back there," I say. I squeeze his shoulder, and he finally reaches up and puts his hand on top of mine. His fingers shake. "I promise you, okay? You're my brother now. You're safe."

He looks back at me and smiles.

"Thanks," he says. "For everything."

I smile back, and then, because I don't know what else I could say, I go back to my homework. He goes back to his game. I can't focus, and not because of the explosions and music on the screen.

If Kyle truly saw a snake—one that definitely wasn't just a normal snake—then it means that none of us are safe.

I consider texting April, partly because she's my girlfriend and I tell her everything, and partly because I want to warn her. I stop myself, though.

There's no use worrying her; she already has enough on her mind. This time last year, I spent the entire week before and after Halloween at her place, trying to distract her from the panic attack she was always at risk of falling into. I don't think she'd been truly convinced that the clown wasn't returning until we finally made it to Thanksgiving. Even then, she made me accompany her to the graveyard where it all began, just to ensure that the tombstone we'd been led to—the tombstone that had eventually opened into a tunnel leading to the clown's lair—was still missing. A memory. Just like the nightmares from the year before.

Besides, of all our fears, Kyle's was the easiest to mistake for reality. It could have been a real snake. It could have also been Kyle's tired imagination.

The clown isn't coming back.

It can't be.

Andres

I wake up covered in sweat, panting, and it takes a long time for the dreams—the nightmares—to settle. Dreams of being stranded in the middle of the ocean. Nightmares of shark fins circling me, closing in . . .

"Eww!" says Marco from the doorway. He's dressed up as a giant pickle. "Why are your sheets all wet? Did you pee the bed?"

"Get out!" I yell, throwing a pillow at him. My younger brother runs away, giggling, clearly already hopped up on stolen candy.

I roll over, but he's right—my sheets are drenched from sweat. *Gross.* I haven't had a nightmare that bad since . . . well, since the clown made all of our nightmares reality. Two years ago, when we went to the graveyard at midnight on Halloween, we found a tombstone that told us to dig. Not our wisest decision, but we did it. We didn't find anything apart from an empty box, but what we released was beyond our worst nightmares.

A monster that showed us what we feared the most.

For me, it was sharks. For Deshaun, it was ghosts. Kyle was haunted by snakes and Caroline by being buried alive. And April . . . she got the worst of it. She was terrorized by the blue-eyed, sharp-toothed clown. It followed her everywhere, tormenting her, a monster even the rest of us could see on occasion. It had nearly dragged us all to the graveyard to feed on our fears for eternity.

Except we managed to band together. We followed it to its lair and faced our fears and locked it away in a casket for good. Since then, life had returned to normal.

So why, as I lie here, can't I get my heart to stop racing? Why does it feel like those horrible days when everything was a waking nightmare? It's stupid, but I honestly expect to see a shark fin gliding by my bed.

My mom knocks on the door.

"Andres?" she asks. "You're going to be late for school. Breakfast is getting cold."

My two other brothers, Lucas and Hector, run past, throwing candy bars at each other. Mom watches them and sighs in exasperation. "Are you doing anything tonight?" she asks.

"Going to the carnival," I say. "April and the rest are getting together."

My brothers run past once more, all three of them this time, and Hector throws a candy bar at my face. Now that my oldest brother is in college, I get to deal with my younger brothers' antics. Meaning, I'm their new target.

"Boys!" Mom yells as they thunder down the steps. "Sure I can't convince you to take them?" she asks. "You wouldn't even have to return them. Honest."

"Not for all the candy in the world," I reply. The *last* thing I need is to babysit my brothers on the one night all my friends are able to hang out. Especially in a crowded amusement park filled with flashy lights and candy—my brothers would be gone in a minute.

"Besides, I can't let you miss out on another amazing trick-or-treat adventure."

Mom groans. Last year, Hector hid a dozen eggs under his vampire cape—the cape he borrowed from *me*, I might add—and egged his friend's house while Marco and Lucas distracted my parents. They were grounded for a week. Miraculously, they managed to keep all their candy.

"Can't say I didn't try," Mom says, exasperated. Then she turns, spots my brothers doing something else they aren't supposed to be doing, and yells at them to stop or else she'll ban sugar in the house.

I peel myself out of bed and head to the shower. Even though I'm running late, there's no way I'm going to school like this. I smell horrible.

I turn on the shower and watch the water swirl and collect in the bottom of the tub, once more feeling myself transported back to the nightmares, back to the horrible events of two years ago. Being lost at sea. Swimming as hard as I could from a shark. A shark that appeared in this very tub . . .

I shake my head.

"That was years ago," I tell myself as I step under the spray. "It's over. It's all over."

The school day passes in a blur. It's clear even our teachers aren't focusing or trying to get us to learn. We end up watching the original *Frankenstein* in English class, and in history we're tasked with researching our favorite scary myths and where they're from, which is actually a lot of fun.

I sit with April and Caroline at lunch. The cafeteria is also attempting to be festive—there are plastic cauldrons of pumpkin-shaped cakes and candy on each of the tables, though the main food is as gross as ever. Lasagna. At least they didn't try stuffing it with candy corn.

"Are you excited for tonight?" Caroline asks.

I nod and grab another handful of candy. The pasta is hard as a rock and I've given up on being healthy today. It's a holiday, after all.

Caroline's wearing a skeleton onesie, her blonde hair in two pigtails with plastic bone ties, and April is dressed as a zombie, with mottled gray skin and heavy shadows under her eyes.

I didn't have time to change into my costume this morning.

"What are you going as?" Caroline asks me.

"A clown," I say flatly.

April drops her fork. "Andres—"

"I'm kidding!" I reply, throwing up my hands. "I'm going as a shark. Kyle's going to be a pirate. Got him a talking parrot for his shoulder and everything."

Caroline snorts. "That's so cute. Are you sure you're okay going as a shark?"

"Yes," I say, sitting up tall. "I'm owning my fears. After all." I then recite what I've forced myself to research. "The fear of sharks is totally unrealistic and fueled by the media. They are a beautiful, necessary part of the ocean's ecosystem, and without them the entire planet would crumble. Nothing to be scared about. Even if they do have giant teeth." I shudder dramatically—it's only partway theatrical. The rest of me is still admittedly scared.

April smiles, which looks gruesome because she went so far as to put black on her teeth. "Well, I can't wait to see. I think Deshaun is going to go as a zombie as well."

"Aww, the two couples planned out their costumes together," Caroline says.

I grin, feeling my cheeks blush. But the flush goes away when April speaks.

"I don't want to ask, but no one got any notes, right?"

I shake my head. So does Caroline.

"Okay, good," April says. "I texted Deshaun and he didn't get one either. Neither did Kyle." Her gross smile widens. "Which is good. One more year without the clown."

"I feel like that deserves a cheer," I say. I grab my milk carton, and the girls raise theirs. "To another year of being clown free."

We tap cartons and drink. Once more, I'm reminded of my nightmares, and I wonder if the girls had similar bad dreams or if it was just stress, but before I can ask, a hand clamps down hard on my shoulder.

"Andres!"

I jolt and look around.

"Oh, hey, Jeremy, how's it going?"

Jeremy's on the soccer team with me. He's tall and fast, definitely one of the cool kids, which has always made me wonder why he hangs out with me. Right now, he's dressed as a vampire, though I can see his freckles through the pasty makeup he's wearing.

"Doing all right," he says. "Are you guys going to the carnival tonight? It's gonna be sick."

"Of course," I reply. "We've got a group going."

"Right on. I gotta take my little brother and his friends. See you guys there?"

I nod.

Then he turns around and joins his definitely-more-popular-than-us friends at their table.

"I still think it's so weird that he's your friend now," April says. "I mean, he's, like, super cool."

"And I'm not?" I reply. "I think I'm offended."

"Please, you don't have enough pride to be offended," April says, throwing a piece of candy corn at me. Her grin falters as she looks over at Jeremy's table. "I realized this morning that they're setting up the carnival right outside the cemetery. So many kids near the graveyard . . ."

"Relax," I say. "It's fine. It's over. Remember? No notes today. No waking nightmares. It's all fine."

"I wish I could believe you," April says.

I try to keep my smile on firmly, but her uncertainty gets under my skin. Even as Caroline chips in and starts talking about what movies we should watch at her place tomorrow night, I can't stop feeling like maybe April is right to be worried.

I think of my dreams.

Of waking up convinced I was stuck in the ocean with sharks circling me.

When I take another drink of my milk, I realize my hands are shaking.

Caroline

"Wow," Andres says. "This place is intense."

The five of us stand just outside the entrance to the carnival. I can't actually remember the last time we all hung out like this. I think we had a sleepover at April's house on her birthday last year. That couldn't have been the last time, could it? In any case, tonight will definitely make up for it.

Flashing lights and organ music and happy (or terrified) screams beckon us forward, along with the scent of cotton candy and popcorn. But we don't move. We stand there, twenty feet from the arched entryway, stunned.

Not just because the carnival is absolutely packed with people.

The striped, neon-lit archway leading to Cheery Charlie's Carnival is topped with a giant, blue-eyed, smiling clown head.

I try to tell myself that it doesn't look anything at all like the clown that haunted us, the clown we buried in the graveyard that stretches up on the other side of the road, but it's difficult. At least this clown head doesn't seem evil.

"Why in the world did they decide to set up by the graveyard?" April asks. She holds Deshaun's hand tight. Their matching zombie outfits are adorable. In a creepy sort of way.

Andres shrugs. "Empty lot?"

It definitely adds an extra layer to the creep factor of the place. On one side of the road, the graveyard sweeps out under the moonlight in rolling hills and gnarled trees, all shadows and bad memories. That is where my mother is buried. That is where we got rid of the clown.

On the other side, blinking wildly, is the carnival, filled with life and light and noise. The two scenes

couldn't be more opposite . . . yet they feel connected. As if the carnival couldn't have been built
anywhere else.

As if it were meant to be right here, side by side
with the dead, right next to our worst nightmares.

Chills race across my skin as I stare at the entrance.

For some reason, I suddenly want to go in there as
much as I'd want to go to the graveyard alone. Farther
in, I see someone dressed as a clown, beckoning kids
inside.

"Is that . . . ?" April asks with a shudder.

"No," Andres says. "Definitely not."

The clown in question is wearing a big polka-dot
outfit, with fluffy pink hair like cotton candy and a
big pink smile.

"Are you sure this is a good idea?" April asks.
Her gaze goes from the clown to the graveyard as she
says it.

Maybe it's my imagination, but when I follow her
gaze, I hear a voice. The faintest whisper.

Come play, Caroline. I miss you, Sunnybunny.

No.

No, it's just my imagination.

"Come on," I say. I take April's hand. "It will be better inside."

I don't know if it's true, but at least in there, we're surrounded by music to drown out the whispers, and lights to burn away the shadows.

At least in there, we're surrounded by the living rather than the dead.

Kyle

I want to be enjoying myself. Really, I do. But crowds are, like, my least favorite thing in the world. Especially crowds of screaming children. And I'm not a big ride person. I get sick easily. Like the rest of us, I'm not a clown person either—and, lucky us, it seems like all the workers here are dressed as clowns. So the carnival is the last place I want to be.

If it weren't for the huge grin on Andres's face when we all step through the archway, I'd have probably turned around and gone home. But he looks truly happy, and especially dorky in his giant shark onesie. That helps me forget where we are. So I push down my discomfort and try to look like I'm enjoying myself. At least I'm dressed as a pirate—if anyone catches me scowling, I can just pretend I'm being in character.

We head straight past a clown making balloon animals and go to a booth to buy some cotton candy.

"I haven't had this in *ages*," Andres says, pulling off a blue tuft and shoving it in his mouth.

"As if you need any more energy," I say, grinning. He gives me a shove, then pulls off a piece of cotton candy and stuffs it in my mouth.

"What do you think we should do first?" Caroline asks as she eats her own cotton candy.

"Tilt-A-Whirl!" April calls out.

"Really?" I ask. "Doesn't that make you want to hurl?"

"Only if I've eaten a lot," she says with a grin. "Which means we should do it *now*, before bingeing on hot dogs and popcorn."

"Blegh," I say. "I can't. I'll throw up. But you guys can go. I'll watch."

April's face drops.

"Okay," she says. "It's not as fun if we don't all go."

I shrug uncomfortably. "Sorry. I can't really do rides."

"How about you guys go?" Andres suggests, nodding to April and Deshaun and Caroline. "Kyle and I will go do our own thing and meet you in, like, ten?"

"Um, yeah, if you want," April says.

"Come on, let's Tilt-A-Whirl," Deshaun says. He doesn't look very excited about going on the ride either—I know for a fact that he also gets nauseated on rides, but he seems ready to test his luck for April's sake. "I'm starving and want to get this over with. See you guys on the other side!"

The three of them skip off, leaving Andres and me standing in the middle of the boulevard, lights flashing and families racing all around us.

"So, um, what do you want to do?" Andres asks me.

I glance around. I don't want to just stand here while everyone else is having fun.

"Maybe we could do the balloon darts?" I say. I force myself to smile. "You can try to win me a prize."

He jumps up and down excitedly, his fins flopping about. *Ridiculous.* My smile becomes real.

"Okay," he says. "But if I win one of the really big prizes, I'm keeping it. Also you have to play, and if you win anything, I get to keep that too." He smiles his big, goofy grin, and my earlier discomfort fades away. That smile always makes me feel better.

I chuckle. "Deal."

We head over to the booth, where a bored-looking teen in a Cheery Charlie's Carnival T-shirt and ridiculous clown makeup stands beside a wall of balloons. We pay him, and he gives each of us three darts.

"So," Andres says, aiming his first dart.

"So," I reply.

"Does this count as a date?" He throws his dart and misses.

I throw mine; it grazes a balloon, but it doesn't pop.

"I guess. Why?"

He shrugs and glances over at me. "Because we haven't been on a date in, like, weeks."

I bite my lip and try to focus on the balloons rather than the guilt worming through my guts.

"I know," I reply. "But we've both been really busy. You've had practice and I've had—"

"Plenty of excuses," Andres interjects. He tosses his dart. The balloon pops, and he cheers. "I mean, I'm not blaming you or anything. Just saying you always seem to have a reason not to go out with me. I was starting to think I'd done something wrong."

The guilt grows, becomes acidic. I focus on the balloons in front of me and ready my next dart.

I don't know how to explain to him how I've been feeling lately. Like I'm a stranger in my own skin. Like I'm becoming something or someone I don't want to be.

Like the past is catching up to me, hissing curses in my ear, turning everything happy and good in my life rotten.

Even my relationship with him.

I throw the dart, straight toward a lime-green balloon.

When it pops, something falls out. A looping, coiling band of black, dropping to the dirt below.

A snake.

There was a snake in the balloon.

And yet Andres and the bored teen don't seem to notice. I'm so focused on trying to find it again that I don't even hear Andres cheer when he pops his final balloon.

"I win!" he calls out. He picks out a tiny stuffed pig and holds it to his chest, looking delighted. I wish I could feel happy too, but once more I feel like I'm a step apart.

There wasn't a snake in the balloon. That was impossible. The clown isn't back. I'm just tired.

"Should we play again?" Andres asks.

Before I can answer, I catch sight of Deshaun, April, and Caroline in the crowd. I wave to them.

Caroline and April are grinning, but Deshaun definitely looks a little green.

"How was it?" I ask when they gather around.

"Don't ask," Deshaun says miserably.

April gives him a big side hug. "Poor Deshaun started feeling a little sick on the ride."

"A little?" Caroline giggles. "He ran straight for a trash can the moment we got off."

Deshaun closes his eyes. "Please. I don't want to think about it."

"I take it that means hot dogs are out right now?" I tease.

Deshaun moans.

"We could play another round?" Andres suggests. "I just won a pig, but I could upgrade to a giraffe if we win again."

Even though I'm trying to smile, I can't stop thinking about the snake I swear I saw fall out of the balloon. The snake that could be slithering around our feet at this very moment.

I don't really want to stay here. The more I stand in one place, the louder the hissing becomes.

"How about the hall of mirrors?" I say, pointing farther off. "That's not too intense for Deshaun's poor stomach."

The others agree, and we make our way to the hall of mirrors.

The building is long and flat, and the walls are glass and angled mirrors, so we can see some of the kids already making their way through the maze inside. We pay the kid at the entrance and go in, one at a time.

The moment I'm in the maze, the music and madness from outside fades away, becomes a distant blur. A distant hiss. The mirrors and glass panes warp my vision. I can see flickering lights outside and the shadows of the others in the maze, as well as my reflection. I can't tell if the wandering shadows are my friends or strangers. I walk slowly, arms outstretched so I don't run into anything, and start to wonder if this was really a good idea.

Yes, I needed to be away from the noise, but in

here, I'm surrounded by myself, and that's almost worse.

Especially because in here, the music and screams of delight from outside are replaced by even louder hissing.

I turn a corner and see the blurry form of Andres farther in. I wave, but he doesn't see me. That makes my heart drop . . . and the hissing grows louder. Along with the voice I've tried so hard to drown out.

He doesn't like you, whispers my father. *He could never like you. He's already growing bored. Just like your other friends. You're no fun. You're not like them.*

I walk faster, but my father's voice follows, along with the hissing that I can no longer drown out. I have to get out of here. Have to find my friends. My hands slap against mirrors and clear walls, my reflection bouncing back into infinity everywhere I turn.

They won't be your friends for much longer, comes my father's voice. *Not when they realize who you are. Not when they see who you've become.*

I turn the corner

and come face-to-face with myself. My true self.

I freeze.

And stare at my reflection.

Me, but I'm no longer me. No longer staring at a scrawny boy with choppy black hair and sad eyes. I'm older. Angrier.

I look like my father.

Snakes slither around my feet. A huge white boa with burning blue eyes drapes around my shoulders.

I stumble backward, but the reflection doesn't waver, doesn't move.

He smiles. His mouth splitting wide. His eyes turning cruel. Turning blue.

You can't escape what you are, my reflection says.

Then the reflection changes.

Shifts.

My skin goes chalk white. Black diamonds of ink cover my eyes. My teeth grow sharp. My pirate outfit becomes puffy and striped . . .

My reflection becomes the clown.

I've missed playing with you, Kyle, the clown says. It reaches out, the white boa wrapping around its arm, the snake's tongue flicking, searching, hunting for me. The snake slithers from the mirror . . .

I don't keep watching. I turn and run, stumbling through the halls, slamming against more mirrors.

I don't stop running until I get out into the welcoming chaos of the carnival, the music and laughter and lights.

But as I wait there for my friends to return, my breath hot in my chest, I know the clown is right.

I can't escape what I am.

Not anymore.

Deshaun

If it wasn't for my love of April and a little bit of social pressure, I probably would have left right after the Tilt-A-Whirl. I feel like I'm spinning even while standing on solid ground. The hall of mirrors doesn't help at all; staring at reflections of myself only makes my concept of space and time falter. By the time I make it out, all I want to do is curl up into a ball and close my eyes and sleep. But everyone else is having fun, so I try to force myself to stay in the game.

"What are you thinking?" Andres asks the group over nachos and hot dogs—I'm abstaining from everything but water, but even that is making my stomach lurch. "Games, or another ride?"

The thought of another ride makes the lurching worse. I take slow, steady breaths and focus on the solid bench beneath me.

April puts a hand on my shoulder.

"Are you feeling okay?" she asks.

I shrug.

"We don't have to go on any more rides," she says.

"No, it's okay, I want you guys to have fun."

I really don't want to ruin her night; I know how much she was looking forward to this, how much she needed a night of us all being together. I don't want to be the reason it falls apart.

Before I can worry too much, a group of kids comes up to us. I recognize Jeremy, but the others are younger. I don't think I've seen them around before.

"Hey, guys," Jeremy says. He's wearing a devil outfit and bumps fists with Andres. "This is my little brother Caleb." He claps his hand on the shoulder of the boy wearing a bright orange hat—I think he's supposed to be a lumberjack. "I'm on babysitting duty tonight. These are Caleb's friends Eliza"—the girl with pigtails and braces and a witch costume waves—"and Kerrie and Kevin Bronson. They're twins, obviously." The two redheaded kids grin awkwardly, which is terrifying given the fact that they're both dressed like clowns.

I realize that they were the kids standing next to us on the playground yesterday. Small world.

"We just got here," Jeremy says. "Do you guys want to go on some rides together?"

"I was actually feeling kinda tired," Kyle says. He glances at me. Ever since he got out of the hall of mirrors, he's been even moodier than usual. "I think Deshaun and I are going to go home. But you all can hang out together?"

Andres and April both cast him a confused look, then nod slowly. Caroline seems on the fence. I don't say anything; I don't want to admit it, but going home right now sounds perfect. I have a horrible feeling that if we do anything else—even a game—I'm going to hurl again.

"If that's what you want to do," Andres says, sounding a little defeated.

Kyle doesn't meet his gaze. "Yeah, I'm not feeling too hot. You know I'm not a ride person."

"Okay, well," April says, trying to sound cheerful. She looks at me, then gives me a quick hug and kisses me on the cheek. "Have a good night. Feel better. I'll text you later."

I nod. It feels awkward leaving like this, but I'm also incredibly grateful to Kyle for taking the fall. I know he's not having the best time, but I also know he would have stuck it out if not for me feeling so nauseated.

We part ways, Kyle giving Andres a quick good-bye hug, and then Kyle and I make our way through the crowded lanes of the carnival, neither of us saying anything.

It's not until we've passed under the archway and stepped out into the cool night air that I break the silence.

"You didn't have to do that," I say. Even talking makes my stomach twist, which makes me grateful that Kyle's never been the super-talkative sort.

He shrugs.

"I wasn't really feeling it, anyway."

I glance over to him.

"Are you jealous of Jeremy?" I ask.

"No," he says quickly. "Why?"

"It's just that you seemed kinda upset when he showed up."

Kyle doesn't answer at first.

"Jeremy's everything I'm not," he says. "He's out-going and cheerful and athletic."

"And you think Andres would like that more?"

"I don't know what I think. I just know I can't compete with that."

"You don't have to," I say.

Kyle just shrugs again.

We make our way home, passing by houses with toilet-papered trees or flickering pumpkins. Trick-or-treat ended a few hours ago, but we occasionally cross a group of kids in costume, eating candy from bags and buckets or trying to scare stragglers. I want to comfort Kyle, but I can't think properly with my stomach doing somersaults.

When we reach the house, we say goodnight and go to our rooms.

I head to the bathroom and remove the zombie makeup, then take some stomach meds for good measure.

We've gone all day without any sight of the clown. No notes. No nothing.

Another year, and the clown is still gone.

Another year, and we're still safe.

I walk around my bedroom, quickly checking all my defenses just for good measure, making sure the crystals are still under the mattress, and the salt still beside the windows and doors. Then I light a candle and some incense, trying to cleanse the air like I've read about. Just in case.

Because even though I know we're safe, I'm still not willing to believe it.

I text April that we're home, that I hope they have fun. She responds with a kissing emoji. And then I turn on my game system and play for a while, until my stomach stops feeling gross and I start feeling tired.

Eventually, I turn off the light and close my eyes. I can hear Kyle watching a movie in his bedroom. A part of me wonders if I should go in there, but I know him better than anyone else. Like me, he gets in his head really easily. And like me, the best thing to do in that case is to just leave him alone, even though I feel guilty doing it.

But it's okay. He only had a bad night. The clown is gone.

We're safe.
We're safe.

I wake with a start.

I'd been having a nightmare.

It was night.

In the graveyard.

And I had been running from something.

Something with burning blue eyes and sharp teeth.

I try to remember what it was, but the harder I think about it, the more the nightmare fades.

"Just a dream," I whisper to myself. *Just a dream*.

I close my eyes and roll onto my side, trying to get back to sleep. I have a math quiz in the morning. Heaviness starts to settle in . . .

Chills race down the back of my neck. I'm being watched. I know it.

My blood goes cold. A part of me wonders if it's Kyle, playing a prank, but the moment I think that, I realize he'd never do something that mean. Especially not on a night like this.

You have to face your fears, I tell myself. We learned that lesson the hard way.

I open my eyes and turn to face the window.

Just in time to see two pale blue eyes watching me, a needle-sharp smile glowing in the clown's shock-white face.

I blink.

The clown vanishes.

But there, in the frost on the window, are scratched three terrifying words:

TIME TO PLAY

April

When I wake up the next morning, I know that something is wrong.

I know this as surely as I know that the sky outside is clear blue. Because the moment I wake up, I'm covered in sweat and panting like I've run a thousand miles.

Like I've spent those thousand miles running from a clown.

The very thought sends chills down my arms, a cold that makes my sweat turn to ice. I can't remember my dreams, but that doesn't mean I'm not scared by them.

Sometimes, it's the things you can't see that are worse.

For a split second, I consider texting Deshaun. I don't know what I'd say, though. *I had a bad dream. I think the clown is back.*

There's no use scaring him over nothing.

I flop back in bed and stare at the ceiling, trying to slow my breath and let the sun warm me. Birds chirp happily outside. Downstairs, I can hear my little brother, Freddy, singing at the top of his lungs while he eats breakfast.

After Deshaun and Kyle left last night, we hung out with Jeremy and his brother's friends for another hour or so. We went on a few more rides, and Andres played the balloon dart game, like, a dozen more times until he'd won enough to get a big stuffed giraffe that he was planning on giving to Kyle. Then the two groups separated. Jeremy's group stuck around to go on a few more rides. Caroline and Andres and I walked out the front entrance and stared out at the hills of the graveyard in silence.

I didn't realize my hands were shaking until Andres took one and Caroline took the other.

Clouds had rolled heavily through the sky, and a cold breeze rustled the trees. But the graveyard was silent.

We stood there for a while, watching the shadowy

hills, until a group of kids loudly left the carnival behind us. Caroline's dad drove us all home, and I came in the house to see Freddy still running around in his donut costume, my mom apparently having given up getting him to bed. I had no such problem; even after showering off my zombie makeup, I still felt like the walking dead. I fell asleep immediately.

Now awake, I stare at the ceiling. It's hard to believe that two years have passed. It feels like it was yesterday. The clown hiding behind every dark corner. The nightmares manifesting as reality.

I reach over and fumble around in my nightstand. Static leaps through my fingers when I find the piece of paper.

I unfold it and stare at it in the morning light, fear creeping through my heart as I read the words I've long since memorized, the note that started this nightmare: *Meet in the graveyard. Tonight. Midnight. Or else.*

Except this time, when I read the note, my heart stutters over the words that simply can't be real.

THEY MET IN THE GRAVEYARD. LAST NIGHT. MIDNIGHT. NOW THEY ARE MINE.

I jolt in shock and sit upright.

That can't be right. Those aren't the right words. Not the words I've read hundreds of times since finding the note in my locker.

Did someone, maybe Freddy—?

But no. I read the note over and over again, and there's no mistaking it. It's the same handwriting. The same creepy black marker. It's most definitely the note from two years ago. Only different.

Someone has changed the note.

But how?

Who?

From my closet, I hear an unmistakable giggle

and jingle of bells.

Andres

"It's happening again," April gasps.

"What is?" I reply. "And why didn't you text me you were on your way?"

She's practically out of breath, *and* she's early. We normally meet at my house and walk to school together, but today she arrived twenty minutes early.

I'm still in my pajamas, and my brothers are racing around the house, yelling and throwing old socks while my parents try to wrangle them to get ready for school. Clearly, they've nearly depleted their store of candy from last night. But my annoyance at my sugar-high brothers is short-lived. Panic is clear on

April's face, and I know there's only one thing in the world that would make her look this scared *and* run all the way to my place.

"There wasn't time to text," she says. She holds out her hand and reveals a crumpled note.

My heart stops when I see it. I know that note well. I received a similar one two years ago.

"Why did you keep that?" I ask, my voice shaking.

"Look at it," she says, pushing it closer to my face.

"I don't want to," I reply. "I already know what it says."

"No," she insists, "you don't."

And she uncrumples the note, holding it out to me.

I read it three times before I can say anything. Every time I read it, my heart drops another foot closer to my toes.

"Did you do this?" I whisper.

She shakes her head.

I've known April for years. We've been through more than most friends ever have. I know when she's pulling my leg. And I know with absolute certainty that this isn't one of those times.

"I found it this morning," she says. "Something

felt wrong when I woke up, and I don't know . . . I grabbed it from the nightstand and, well, you see what it says. *It's changed*. What do you think it means?"

I read it over again, even though I don't need to. The words feel burned into my brain. *They met in the graveyard . . . Now they are mine.*

Did the others meet up without us? I can't imagine Caroline and Kyle and Deshaun heading to the graveyard, but who else could it be talking about? The questions make fresh panic spike through my veins.

"Have you contacted the others?" I ask.

She nods. "I texted them all on my way over. They're all fine."

"Did you say anything about the note?" I ask, trying not to be insulted that she had time to text them, but not me.

She shakes her head.

"I didn't think it was something to text." Her eyes fill with tears. "I just . . . I don't know what to do, Andres. What if it's coming back?"

I step forward and wrap her in a tight hug. Immediately, she starts sobbing onto my shoulder.

Hector runs past, stops, and whistles. I yell at him

to go back inside. He giggles and ducks away before I can swat at him.

"I'm sure—" I begin to say, but I stop myself. I don't like lying. Especially not to April. And right now I'm not sure of anything.

"Here," I continue instead. "Come inside. I'll get ready and we can figure it out on the way to school. Just . . . don't tell anyone else about this yet, okay? Not until we know for sure what's going on. We don't need to scare anyone."

She sniffs and nods and follows me inside. I leave her in the kitchen with my mom, who's packing lunches—it's probably the safest place in the house from my brothers' wildness.

I run upstairs and grab my clothes from my room, yell at my brothers again, and make my way into the bathroom. I fill the sink with water and wash my face. It's the quickest I've ever gotten dressed and ready for school. And that's including the days I've slept in or when my brothers hogged the bathroom until the last minute.

As I drain the water and turn to run back downstairs, I freeze.

No.

It must be my imagination.

It must be April's paranoia getting to me.

But I could swear, just for a moment, from the corner of my eye, I see a gray fin circling in the emptying sink.

Deshaun

It takes all my self-control not to say anything to Kyle when we walk to school together. I want nothing more than to tell him what I saw on the window last night, but I don't want to worry him. It already seems like he has enough on his mind, and besides, it was all probably just my imagination and fear over the whole two-year-mark thing. Kyle walks silently at my side. I mean, he's normally pretty quiet, especially in the morning and *especially* if he hasn't had any coffee—which is the one thing my parents won't budge on, so he always has to grab a cup from the café on the way to school. But today he seems even more withdrawn. Even after the coffee.

I'm in a similar state. It took forever to fall back asleep after seeing the clown last night, and when I did, my sleep was riddled with old nightmares.

Dreams from the time, years ago, I was lost in the graveyard at night. The very graveyard that—years later—led us into this mess. Dreams where I was chased by the ghosts that lingered in old tombstones. Dreams where no matter how hard or fast I ran, I couldn't escape.

The ghosts were always there.

Watching.

Waiting.

"BOO!"

I nearly jump out of my skin as a kid runs past me from behind, laughing with his friends as they hustle toward the school.

Kyle finally seems to jolt out of his introspection. He glares at the kids as they scamper off.

"Little jerks," he growls.

I just sigh and wish I could be as happy as they are. Scaring because it's fun, and not being scared for their lives.

I watch the kids run off around the corner. A moment later, there's a loud, short scream that I recognize immediately as April's. Kyle and I look at each other, and then break into a run.

Andres and April come into sight from behind the fence. Andres is suppressing his laughter and April is bright red.

"It isn't funny!" she says loudly.

"I know, I know," he says.

We slow our jog when we near them—clearly, the kid managed to scare her.

Andres smirks at us. "But," he says, "it *kind of* was."

April's face is starting to lose a little of its reddish tint, but she's still upset—and the moment she starts talking, it's clear why.

"It's back," she says.

Andres stops giggling immediately. He takes a step closer to Kyle, who takes his hand on reflex. I want to reach out to April to comfort her, but I'm in too much shock to move.

"What's back?" I ask. Even though I know. The words scratched onto my window flash through my mind: *TIME TO PLAY.*

I know.

"No," Kyle whispers. He takes a step backward

and stumbles over the curb. Andres helps steady him, and I step closer to help. Kyle shakes his head. "No, no, it can't be back. We banished it. It's over."

April swallows.

"I don't want to believe it either," she says. "But this morning . . . I found this."

She holds up a crumpled note. I know it all too well. Or rather, I *should* know it all too well.

When I read it, it's clear that someone has changed the words.

The *clown* changed the words.

Kyle grabs the note and studies it.

"What's this?" he asks. "Is this some sort of joke?"

"No," April says. Tears well in her eyes. I look between Kyle—my best friend—and April—my girlfriend—and can't decide who to comfort. So I just stand there, silent, feeling completely powerless to help at all. Powerless, just like two years ago.

"I don't believe it," Kyle says. He forcefully hands her back the note. "You rewrote the note. To—I don't know, get us all to be together again. Is that it? Because we've grown apart, you thought it would be cute to pull a prank. Maybe do another trip to the graveyard just for fun. Well, I'm not buying it. It isn't funny."

April tries to stutter out some sort of response, but his tirade washes over her, and the moment he's done, he pushes away Andres's hand and storms off toward the school.

Andres looks between Kyle and April, just as lost as I am.

"Sorry," Andres says. "He's just . . . He didn't . . ." He stalls. Looks back as his boyfriend abandons us. "Sorry."

Then Andres runs after Kyle, calling out for him to stop.

April stands there, tears running freely down her cheeks.

"I believe you," I say after a moment. Probably too long a moment. "Last night, I saw—"

"It doesn't matter," she says angrily. My gut drops—the dismissal stings. She wipes her eyes fiercely and sniffs. "It's already done what it wants to."

"What do you mean?"

"Don't you remember?" she asks, looking at me with watery eyes. "We only defeated it when we banded together. And now all it took was one note, and we've fallen apart. Who knows what it will do next?"

Wind whispers through the trees. The rattle of branches.

The growl of my name.

I swear I feel the clown watching from the bare treetops, but I don't look. I won't look. I shudder and take April's hand. She doesn't squeeze back.

"Come on," I say. "We'll catch up to them. I'm sure he's just upset because he doesn't want to believe we're in danger. But he'll listen to us. I know he will. There was writing on my window last night, April. And Kyle admitted that he saw a snake yesterday. I'm sure he's just in denial. He doesn't want to believe it's back."

"I don't either," she says. "But we don't have a choice."

She starts walking toward the school. I follow, but as I go, I look over my shoulder to a group of kids on the sidewalk. One of them stands a little taller than the rest. My blood goes cold when I see him.

The pale blue eyes.

The terrible, snakelike smile.

The pearly white face.

The clown.

The clown waves at me, the gesture menacing.

Then I blink, and it's just a kid. Just a normal, makeup-free kid.

I wish I could convince myself that's all it ever was.

Kyle

"Kyle, wait!" Andres calls from behind me.

But I don't slow down.

I don't wait.

If I do, I know I'll see them, slithering through the leaves.

If I do, I know I'll be back in the nightmare I fought so hard to overcome.

"Kyle!"

Andres grabs my arm and forces me to a halt. I spin on the spot and glare at him, but he doesn't let go. For a moment, for a brief, terrible moment, a voice roars inside my head, telling me to throw him off, to shove him away.

A voice that sounds far too much like my father's.

I force it away and try to calm down.

I'm not going to become like my dad. I'm not.

You already are.

"What's going on?" Andres asks.

I swallow hard and look down to my feet. I almost expect serpents to slither over my shoes, but I see only my sneakers and the pavement.

"It can't be back," I say. "We banished it. This is all just some, I don't know, cry for attention."

"Dude—"

"You heard April! She's sad that we don't hang out anymore, so she's making up stories to get us back together again. Maybe she got the idea at the carnival last night, thought it was the best way to keep us together. It's not right."

"You know that's not true," Andres whispers.

"You just can't see it because she's your best friend," I reply. There's an edge to my voice I can't shake, an anger that simmers.

"Look, none of us want to believe this is happening. But what's the harm in being prepared?"

"We scare ourselves and make something out of nothing."

"Or we're on alert and prevent something worse from happening." Andres pauses and looks back toward Deshaun and April, who have passed to the other side of the street to walk past us. "They're our friends," he continues. "We have to stick together. You know what happened last time. The only reason we got out of that grave was because we were a team. We can't let this split us apart."

I want to agree with him. I know it's logical and rational, but the more I stand and listen to him lecture, the more my dad's anger builds inside me and the more I want to scream at him to shut up.

"We know what to expect," he says calmly. "We know what to look out for. Our fears—"

"You don't know anything about fear!" I shout. Suddenly I'm no longer standing outside.

I'm standing in the basement of my old house, my dad behind me, his hands on my shoulders, forcing me to stay put. We stand in the center of the room, the space lit by a single bare bulb above, its light casting harsh shadows over the dozens of snakes hissing and coiling in the terrariums around me. The sound of their slithering does nothing to drown out my dad's warning: *This is what you get for trying to stand up to me. Don't make a noise. Don't move a muscle. Or I'll let them out and lock you in here.*

"Kyle," Andres whispers. "Kyle, what's wrong?"

His voice snaps me from the memory. Except it's not Andres staring at me anymore.

It's my dad. Standing on the sidewalk outside our school. His eyes burning bright blue, just like the clown's. His smile stretched in a sinister sneer. Snakes spill from between his serrated teeth.

I don't answer him.

I turn and run for the school, serpents hissing in my wake.

Caroline

I didn't sleep at all last night. Bad dreams. Nightmares. I blamed it on all the cotton candy and soda at the carnival, all the bright lights and rides. A sleepless night explains the dark shadows under my eyes and the tremor in my fingers as I get ready, the gross churning in my stomach and the ache in my temples.

But it doesn't explain why everything feels different as I walk to school. Muted. Like a waking dream.

I've had sleepless nights before. All-nighters for tests. Bingeing shows on my computer. A few girls-only slumber parties with April. But I've never felt like this.

At least, not since we banished the clown. Not since my nightmares of being buried alive ended.

I almost asked my dad to drive me. But he's busy with work and I don't want to bother him. Plus I like the freedom. For some reason, walking makes me feel closer to my mother. She loved wandering around. We'd often drive out to the countryside and go on all-day walks through the fields and forests. They're my favorite memories of her, before illness took her away.

And even though I'm lost in my thoughts, something pulls at me. More of a sensation than a sound. A tug. An urge.

A scent.

And it reminds me so strongly of my mother, I know I have to follow.

Almost without meaning to, I find myself at the edge of town. Near the hill. Near the carnival.

Near the graveyard.

A part of me knows I should keep going. School starts in twenty minutes and I don't want to be late. But that part is muted. Soft. Like *it* is the part of me that's dreaming, and the rest is wide, wide awake.

Mom's perfume carries on the breeze that winds its way down from the cemetery hill. I follow.

Up past the old iron fence.

Up through the trees with their gnarled, bare branches.

Past the tombstones covered in leaves.

To the very top.

Around the back.

To the ancient tree that stands like a skeleton against the pale blue sky.

To the unmarked grave that waits there.

The grave that spelled so much horror.

The grave that definitely wasn't there when I was here last week.

I freeze before it.

The perfume fades, and so, too, does my certainty. The belief that this was okay. Safe.

Suddenly, the fragrant breeze becomes cold and harsh. The scent changes. Becomes bitter, like decayed animals and rusted metal. I shudder, pull my light coat tighter around me.

"I should go," I say to no one, and turn.

The leaves rustle,

revealing something bright and orange beneath them.

I hesitate.

I should go. I don't know why I came out here.

This isn't my mother's grave. This is where we first unearthed the clown's evil.

This is the grave that vanished when we got rid of the clown.

I shouldn't be here.

And neither should this grave.

But I am. And it is. And there, among the leaves, is a bright orange hat.

I pick it up and examine it. It's familiar, but I don't know why. I shove it in my pocket. It feels important.

Before I can change my mind and toss the hat back to the leaves, I head in the direction of school.

As I cross over the hill and the grave fades from view, I look back over my shoulder.

To see new paint splattered over the tombstone, spelling out the words

HERE LIE THE BODIES OF

I turn away before I can read the names.

I don't want to know.

I don't want to know.

Andres

"Did you hear?" April asks, cornering me in the lunchroom.

So far, Kyle hasn't said another word to me—not that he'd have much chance, seeing as we're in completely different classes. I can't stop thinking about how hurt he looked this morning, how angry. He almost sounded like a different person. It stings. But I know deep down he just needs time. Not even Deshaun has said *hey* in passing. Caroline and I had an English class together, but she sat in the back, looking lost and somewhat haunted. I wanted to ask her what was wrong; she left before I got the chance.

April's the first of my friends who's actually sought me out. I can tell from the expression on her face, however, that I'm not going to like what she's talking about.

"Hear what?" I ask.

She steps in close. The lunchroom is crowded and people are yelling and no one is paying attention to the two of us, but she lowers her voice, anyway.

"Jeremy, his brother, and his brother's friends have gone missing."

I swear my blood freezes.

"What?" I whisper back.

She nods and looks around. Her eyes have a manic, bloodshot haze to them. I wonder when she found out. I wonder how long this has been eating at her.

"I overheard some seniors talking. One of them said that Jeremy and his brother didn't come home last night. Neither did his brother's friends." She pauses and looks at me meaningfully. "Think about it: The last time we saw them, they were at the carnival. By the graveyard. And there were five of them."

"You don't think . . . ?" I begin, but before either of us can say anything, April stands up and looks over my shoulder. I look too, to see Caroline walking our way, her hands behind her back.

"Caroline!" April says, her voice forcefully chipper. "How are you doing? Excited for the sleepover tonight?"

Caroline smiles slightly, but it doesn't stick.

"I went to the graveyard this morning," she says. No introduction. It's a second punch to the gut in five minutes. "I don't know why. I just felt pulled. And . . . the grave was there again." There's no need to ask which one. There's only one grave I know of that could disappear once its contents had been beaten. "There was also . . . this."

She holds out her hands.

I gingerly take the orange hat and hold it in front of me.

"This was Caleb's," I say. I look between them. "Jeremy's little brother. The one dressed as a lumberjack."

"What was it doing by the grave?" Caroline asks.

"None of them came home last night," April says. She fishes in her pocket and pulls out the crumpled note. "And this morning, well . . ." She unfolds it and lets Caroline read. Caroline's jaw drops.

"It's what I feared," Caroline whispers. "As I was turning to go . . . there were words on the tombstone. I didn't see the names. But it said . . . *Here lie the bodies.*"

"No," I whisper. "It can't have gotten them. We saw them last night!"

April shakes her head, tears forming in her eyes.

"It must have gotten to them at the carnival, after we left. I bet it was watching us the whole time." She takes a deep, steadying breath, but her voice still shakes when she speaks again. "If it got Jeremy and the others, we have to try to save them. Otherwise . . ."

"Otherwise, it's going to come after us next," I finish. I look at the hat in my hands.

A small, terrible part of me wonders if it's already too late.

April texts Deshaun immediately after that, and I send one to Kyle as well, though I don't really know what to say. He was already touchy talking about the clown earlier—what will he think when he finds out Jeremy is gone? Surely, he'll have to believe us. Right? What other option is there? I keep my text to the point:

Jeremy, his brother, and his brother's friends went missing. We think it's the clown.

He probably won't get it until the end of the school day anyway, but at least it feels like doing something. Which is more than I can say for the rest of the lunch period. We all three sit there, barely eating, lost in our thoughts.

"We have to help them," April says a few minutes before the final bell rings. "Jeremy and the others. If they were taken by the clown, we have to figure out how to get them back."

"Maybe they're still in the graveyard?" I ask, remembering the night we were trapped in the cave beneath the tombstone.

Caroline shakes her head. "I didn't see any sign of them besides the hat. If they were taken, I don't know how we're going to get them back. The clown isn't just going to give them up easily."

"But we have to do *something*," April says. "Maybe their parents would know . . ."

But she trails off. We all know the truth—the clown isn't going to give anyone back. The clown isn't going to let us find them. It has powers we can't even dream of. There's nothing anyone's parents could do, and no authorities would ever believe us. I mean, come on: Who would believe a group of high schoolers swearing some evil paranormal clown had taken five kids from a town where literally nothing bad has ever happened?

Still, April's right—we have to try *something*.

"Maybe we can swing by the graveyard tonight," I say. "Kyle won't like it, but I bet the five of us together could discover something."

"That feels like walking into a trap," Caroline whispers. "The clown wants us."

"No," I say. "Think about it: If the clown wanted us, it would have gotten us. We were all at the carnival last night. And the clown hasn't gone after us—it chose Jeremy and the rest. Maybe because it knew we would resist. Maybe it was, I don't know, scared of us."

April laughs. "*That* I find hard to believe."

"The clown wants us to be scared," I say. "It's taking people close to us to make us worried. So we just have to be *not* scared. We know its tricks and we know how to defeat it. We'll go to the graveyard and find the others and help them defeat whatever night-mare they're fighting and then put the clown to rest. Again."

Even as I say it, I know it's too simple. The clown won't fall for that trick again. April and Caroline nod, but I can tell that they too don't quite believe me. But neither of them can come up with anything else. My only hope is that Deshaun can think of something bet-ter. I know for a fact that he's spent the last two years trying to problem-solve for every possible threat.

I can't help but wonder if the possibility that the clown would target us by stealing other kids ever crossed his mind.

"Keep your phones on you at all times," April says when the lunch bell rings. "If there's an emergency—even if you just think you saw some-thing strange—text."

"Our phones will get taken away," I say, then real-ize how stupid a worry it is before April even opens her mouth. "Never mind."

"This is important. If you're in trouble, run. No matter what. If the clown is back, if it already took some kids . . . we have to believe it's stronger than ever. We have to believe it has some new tricks up its sleeve."

Caroline shudders at the thought, but we all nod.

"I've told Deshaun and Kyle what we've learned. They haven't responded, but they're still in class. If you see them, warn them. We have to stick together, got it?"

"Got it," I say. I'm instantly reminded of her tears earlier this morning, when she saw how easily just the thought of the clown had created a rift. I have to hope Kyle will see sense. He has to.

The bell rings again. April hugs both of us, then dashes off to class.

"Did you want to keep this?" I ask Caroline, holding up the hat I've been clutching. She shakes her head and leaves me with it.

I don't want to keep it. I consider handing it in to the security officer—after all, it counts as evidence, right? But they won't be able to do anything, even if they did believe us. No normal weapon could defeat the clown. No cops or search dogs could hunt it down.

Just us.

I head over to the nearest trash can and toss the hat inside.

Something rustles within.

I hesitate. Every nerve in my body is set to run, but I take a step closer to the garbage can. Peer into the shadows and wrappers and old food piled inside.

Moments later, the garbage rustles, and hundreds of hairy black spiders crawl out. They scuttle up and over the sides of the can, all shapes and sizes, some as big as my hand.

I yelp and jump back, but the moment I blink, the spiders are gone.

I stand there, staring at the empty trash, my hand clutched to my hammering heart. A few kids laugh at me as they pass, but I barely notice them.

The hat is nowhere to be seen.

What was that? I think to myself.

The spiders were scary, sure, but only because they shocked me, only because there were so many of them. I've never been scared of spiders. Heck, I once asked my parents for a pet tarantula. (They said no. My mom actually *screamed* no.)

Before, we were only shown our deepest fears. Mine is sharks.

So why am I seeing spiders?

I don't have an answer, but when I turn and jog from the cafeteria, the third bell warning that I'm about to be late to my next class, a thought bubbles up to the surface.

Maybe April is right—maybe taking Jeremy and the others has made the clown stronger. Given it powers we can't even dream of.

Maybe this is no longer about just facing our individual fears.

Maybe now, we have to face everyone else's too.

Deshaun

I'm being followed.

I want to think it's my overactive imagination, some combination of seeing April in tears and Kyle freaking out. And yes, that's probably part of it. But in reality, I know that it's not in my head. I know, because it's the exact same sensation I had in the middle of the night, when I looked out my window and saw the blue-eyed, needle-toothed clown grinning back at me.

Time to Play. Time to Play.

The words churn on repeat in my head as I make my way to the cafeteria. Around me, kids are talking or yelling or laughing, but even though I'm surrounded by people, I feel alone.

Alone, save for the set of eyes that burn on the back of my neck wherever I go.

Thankfully, I spot Kyle at the far end of the cafeteria, sitting by himself and poking at his food. I grab my own lunch—a sub sandwich and chips—and make my way over to him.

He glances up briefly when I sit across from him, then looks back down. There are dark circles under his eyes, like bruises, and maybe it's the light, but he looks older. Much, much older.

Haunted.

"Hey," I say after a few moments pass in awkward silence.

"Hey," he grunts back.

"You okay?"

He shrugs.

I've seen him shut down before, but this feels worse. I know that right now, more than ever, the five of us need to stick together. April is right—we defeated the clown before because we worked as a team and helped one another face our fears. But alone? We don't have a chance.

Especially if the clown has fed.

"About this morning—" I begin.

"I don't want to talk about it," he interrupts. His voice is gruff.

"I know, I know, but look, Kyle, this isn't something April is making up."

"Sure."

"No, it isn't! Last night . . ." I take a deep breath. Once more, I feel eyes on the back of my neck, and fight back the urge to look around. "Last night I . . . I saw it. Outside the window. The clown. He was smiling at me with those terrifying eyes, and he'd written something in the frost on the window. He wrote, *Time to Play.*"

Kyle doesn't say anything.

I stare at him, wondering if he's heard me. Then he looks up slowly, and his haunted eyes are even more grim.

"Sure you did," he says. "Just like I'm sure Jeremy and the others are really missing, and this isn't something that April and Jeremy plotted after you and I went home."

The way he says it makes my stomach drop. He even *sounds* older.

He . . . he sounds like his dad.

"What? You don't believe me?"

"Of course I don't believe you," he responds. "There's no way the clown is back. Jeremy and the others are probably just hiding somewhere, skipping school. I bet April even told you to make up the story about seeing the clown outside. I know you'd do anything for her."

"Kyle, I—"

"No!" He slams a hand on the table, making his utensils rattle. A few kids look over, but he ignores them and rages on, though at least he lowers his voice. "No, no excuses. I'm not falling for it, Deshaun. This is all some stupid prank because April wants us all to be together again. I'm not falling for it. I refuse to believe the clown is back. We defeated it. Okay? Over. Done. We all know it, and this whole thing is just sad. Pathetic."

"But why would she do that? Why would any of us pretend the clown was back?"

"Because to you guys, the clown wasn't real. Not really. You all think this is just a game."

"What—"

"It showed you stupid things like ghosts or sharks. Big deal. That isn't scary. Not really. It showed me . . ." He swallows and shakes his head. "It doesn't matter.

It's over. And I refuse to believe otherwise, got it? So just let it go. The clown isn't back. We aren't all going to magically be best friends again. The world doesn't work like that. Just because April doesn't want to grow up and face reality—"

"Dude!"

"What? It's the truth. She hates that we aren't all hanging out all the time. She hates that we're growing up and going separate directions. And all the rest of you hate it too. You don't want to face the future. You don't want to face the truth."

Anger boils in my veins. I've never wanted to yell at Kyle before, but right now, I do.

"And what truth is that?" I ask through gritted teeth.

He stands up and looks at me.

"We're alone. All of us. And we can't depend on anyone."

Then he grabs his tray and storms from the cafeteria.

I watch him go. Watch him throw most of his food in the trash and head out the door. I'm not the only one.

Someone giggles beside me. I turn slowly, fear freezing my blood, because it can't be here. It can't be.

But there, right beside me, is the clown, wearing its puffy outfit, its blue eyes watching Kyle leave.

Then its head turns to face me, slowly, even though the rest of its body stays still. Its eyes pierce like the sun. Were they ever that bright before?

"One down," it says with a giggle. "Four to go."

It opens its mouth wide, splitting its face in two, a great, gaping black pit of razor teeth that stretches and stretches larger than its body. It leans toward me, snaps down to devour me. I can't move. Can't scream.

And right as it swallows me, right as the darkness becomes everything, the clown explodes in a flurry of confetti and balloons and laughter. Right in the middle of the cafeteria. Right in the middle of a few hundred kids.

None of them seem to have seen a thing.

I sit there, my breath racing, burning in my lungs.

Waiting for it to come back.

Waiting for literally anyone else to say something, to raise the alarm. But no one else has seen the clown, or the balloons that pop when they hit the ceiling, or the confetti that melts when it reaches the floor.

Kyle was right about one thing:

We're alone.

If only he'd been right about the clown.

Caroline

Everything is wrong.

We shouldn't be fighting. Not now. Not ever. But especially not now. Not with five other kids missing. Not when I know it's going to come after us next.

It already has.

I sit with April in the back of the classroom. Chemistry. Our teacher, Mr. Borne, drones on, and I try to take notes, but all I can think about is the anger in Kyle's voice and the fear in April's. Something horrible is going on, and it's not just the clown showing us our fears this time.

Somehow, it's found a way to turn us against one another.

April scribbles away in her notebook beside me. I try to catch her eye, but she ignores me. She isn't angry with me, I know. But she is hurt, and there's nothing I can do to help. It makes me feel helpless. Just as helpless as when we buried my mother.

The moment I think it, I feel it—the crumbling walls, the dirt pressing in on all sides, the light fading as the earth closes in. The old fear of being buried alive.

I take deep, steady breaths and press my hands onto the table, remind myself that it is just my imagination, that I am in school, in chemistry, and I am not being buried alive; it is impossible. The feeling slowly fades. I keep breathing deeply. I keep my mind calm. There is no point panicking. I know this.

Dirt falls on the notebook. Great clumps of brown soil tumble across my fingertips.

It's just your imagination.

Even if the clown is back, even if it can catch us here, all it can do is try to scare me. I can fight it by refusing to be scared. Right?

"You think that will work?" comes a voice right beside me. I know that voice, even though I haven't heard it in two years—it's burned into my memory, a nightmare always at the edge of my awareness. The clown. It giggles ominously. I refuse to look over, refuse to give it power.

"I want to play, Caroline. And you will play with me. You. Will. PLAY."

The ground rattles. Beakers and burners roll off the desks, glass vials shatter to the floor. But still I don't look up. Still I refuse. I can't see April anymore, even though I know she remains beside me. I can't hear her, or anyone else, above the grumbling, roaring earthquake as the classroom collapses around me. I close my eyes. *This is all in your head. This is all in your head.*

The rumbling stops. The sensation of dirt on my shoulders and hands disappears.

There's a hiss, a wheezing of air, and something cold and slimy reaches under my chin.

I gasp and open my eyes as a rotting hand turns my head

to face the zombie sitting right beside me.

It is horrible. Gray-green flesh falling from its skull, rotted teeth that smell like old feet, one eyeball dangling from its socket. April and the rest of my class are nowhere to be seen. Instead, I'm standing in a graveyard covered in fog and broken tombstones. Far, far away from reality. And safety.

The zombie smiles at me and wheezes again, its breath a foul cloud. Its fingers tighten around my chin. Its fingernails dig into my flesh. I feel its broken nails cut my cheek. I force myself not to scream or cry because this is real, *this is real*.

"You can't ignore me anymore, Caroline," it says, its voice horribly similar to the clown's but raspier. "I'm no longer just in your imagination. I've fed. I am everywhere. You can't escape. You ran from me once, but now you all are mine!"

From the corner of my mind I see them—dozens of zombies, shambling toward me with rotting flesh and missing limbs. They claw from the ground, moaning horribly. Another skeletal zombie nears, reaches out, puts its hand on my shoulder, pulls me close to devour me.

I scream. Finally, I scream.

And I'm back.

Back in the classroom. Back beside April. The clown is nowhere to be seen, nor are the zombies.

The whole room is silent. Staring at me. And it's only then that I realize it's because I've been screaming out loud. For real.

I swallow hard and look down, trying to ignore the questioning stares and the laughter of my classmates.

"Are you okay, Caroline?" my teacher asks.

I nod silently and wait for him to resume teaching. Thankfully, after what feels like forever, he does. It takes a lot longer for my classmates to look back to their notes. They don't stop laughing quietly to one another. If only they knew. If only they knew . . .

I reach up and touch my cheek. When I bring my hand away, there are tiny drops of blood from where the zombie's nails pierced my skin.

"What was that all about?" April whispers.

"It was here," I reply through the tears that start falling from my cheeks. Fear pulses within me. "It was right beside me. Only now, it's worse. It's so much worse."

"But I didn't see a thing."

I can't respond. All I can do is cry silently and show her the blood on my fingertips. *It was here, and it's no longer just in our heads.*

It can hurt us.

Somewhere in the distance, I hear the clown giggle, along with the jingle of bells.

April

I can't stop worrying for the rest of the school day.

I keep thinking about Caroline freaking out and saying the clown was in class with us—next to me, yet somehow invisible. At least I finally, *finally* got a text back from Deshaun, which didn't say much beyond *we are okay*. But I don't believe it. It's like every time I blink, I can see Kyle pushing us away as he stormed off. I can hear Caroline screaming. I can see the neon-orange hat she handed to me. I can imagine Jeremy and the others being taken.

But the worst part is that while the rest of my friends suffer, I don't see a thing.

Not since the note this morning, not since the giggling.

It's worse than being personally attacked. The knowledge that the clown is out there, biding its time and preying on my friends. It's hunting them, making me watch as they face terrible nightmares. And I can't do anything about it.

I stand outside the school, waiting to catch sight of my friends as the rest of the school spills out. I hope we're still on for the sleepover tonight. I truly don't want to be alone. I don't think any of us should be. It isn't safe.

I almost sigh in relief when Andres and Caroline step out together . . . though Deshaun and Kyle are nowhere to be seen. My heart thuds painfully, and I can't tell if it's relief that Andres and Caroline are okay, or fear that Deshaun and Kyle might not be.

"Did anything new happen?" I ask the moment they near.

"Hello to you too," Andres says. He glances around nervously. "Yeah. After we left the cafeteria, I saw spiders in the garbage can."

"That's not very strange," I say. There are bugs in the cafeteria all the time.

"*These* were. They were huge. The size of my head." He swallows and looks around once more. "I think . . . I think it's changed. It isn't just showing us what we really fear. I think it's showing what others fear too."

"That would explain the zombies," Caroline whispers.

"Zombies?" Andres asks.

I shudder at the cold breeze that blows past as she fills him in. I swear I hear giggling but try to convince myself it's the crowd of kids rushing by, and not the clown listening in.

"The clown," Caroline continues, looking pale with fear, "I mean, the zombie, whatever . . . it said it had fed."

I can't imagine what that means for Jeremy and the others. I don't want to—it's too horrible. We just hung out with them last night! Have they been consumed by the evil? Trapped forever in the caves? Overtaken by their fears?

Each option seems more horrible than the last.

"Have you heard from Kyle?" I ask, trying to push the thoughts away. "I'm worried about him."

"Me too," Andres admits.

"Do you think the clown is getting to him?" I ask.

"I think it's close," he admits.

"Well," I say, "we're just going to have to make sure Kyle comes tonight."

"Tonight?" Andres asks.

"Tonight. Caroline's. The sleepover."

"Right," he says. "Good luck with that."

"I don't need luck," I say. I look toward the door, to where Deshaun and Kyle are *finally* walking out. "I have Deshaun."

"You're going to need more than that," Andres mutters.

Deshaun and Kyle are deep in discussion—it almost looks like an argument—and although it's clear that Kyle's trying to avoid us, Deshaun steers him our way.

"Hey," Deshaun says sheepishly. "How . . . how are you doing?"

"Besides the fact that we're all being hunted by an evil clown that's already captured five kids?" I ask sarcastically. "Great."

"We don't know that it captured them," Caroline says. "There's still hope."

"Right," I say. "But we also know that we're probably the only ones who could find them."

I expect Kyle to say something biting, something about how he isn't going to help, but he just stands there in sullen silence, looking down at his shoes.

"Are you all coming tonight?" Caroline asks the boys.

"Oh," Kyle mutters. "Um."

"Yes," Deshaun says. He nudges Kyle. "We are. Kyle needed to grab some stuff from home, though."

"Yeah," Kyle quickly says. "I'm going to head there now." He looks to Deshaun, then Andres. "Alone."

"Suit yourself," Andres says with a forced nonchalance.

"Okay, then," Deshaun says. He looks at Kyle nervously. "I'll see you later?"

Kyle nods. Then, without a goodbye, he turns and starts walking home. I want to tell him to stop, that we're safer as a group, but I don't want to set him off. It's more important that he comes to Caroline's. Besides, right now it's daylight, and there are other kids walking along the streets with him. He won't be targeted now.

Then I remember that Caroline was targeted when she was sitting right beside me, and my confidence falters.

"Should we really let him go?" Caroline asks.

"He'll be okay," Deshaun replies. He comes over and takes my hand, gives it a squeeze. Then he forces a smile. "We should run by the store and get some snacks. I bet all the Halloween candy is on sale."

"Yeah," I say, squeezing his hand in return. I watch Kyle go, a sinking feeling in my stomach. "That sounds fun."

"What are we going to do about the others?" Andres whispers. "We can't just leave Jeremy and the rest out there. We have to find them."

"But how?" I ask. "You know how the clown works. It's toying with us. It won't reveal them or where it's hiding unless it wants to be found."

"I know," Andres says. "But I still think we should try."

Deshaun clears his throat. "Maybe we should go to the graveyard later," he says. "If Caroline saw the grave, maybe it's a sign. Maybe we can find something out there."

I know it's the last place he wants to be, seeing as he got lost there when he was a little kid, but he tries to keep his voice strong and brave.

"Or maybe it's a trap," Andres says. Deshaun

raises an eyebrow, and Andres quickly carries on. "But, I mean, I'm with you. Even if it is a trap, I don't want to just wait around for the clown to come find us. Or for Jeremy and the others to get hurt worse than they already are." He watches Kyle turn the corner. "We just have to hope we can make it till then."

"We will," Caroline says. "Together."

Except I know the truth. We all do. The clown has already divided us, and unless we manage to mend the cracks, we won't stand a chance.

Kyle

I take the long way home.

Not home. Not really. To Deshaun's house. To where I stay.

His parents may have taken me in, but it's not mine. Not really. I don't fit in there. I don't fit in anywhere. Never have.

I've always been different. Always been apart.

Dad was right in that at least.

I'll never fit in.

I'll never be loved.

Not really.

I don't know why my feet lead me there. Maybe it's

the dark thread of my thoughts pulling me onward. But it seems like I blink, and I'm there.

One minute I'm with my friends outside the school.

The next, I stand outside my old house. *Home.*

I stand on the other side of the street. Staring up at the curtained windows, dark in the afternoon light. The well-mowed front yard. Normally mowing was my job, but I bet Dad made sure Mom did it. He always did like a clean yard. And a clean house. Even if he refused to be the one making it clean.

Everything is perfect from the outside.

The neat yard cleared of leaves. The single ghost hanging from the porch rafters, just enough to be festive, not enough to invite people in. The white walls and pale blue trim.

A festering wound within.

I stare at the house and wonder at how similar we are, the house and I. Both put together from the outside. A mess on the inside.

I stare, and it seems like darkness seeps in on the edges. Until it's just me and the house, the two of us floating in darkness. Birds of a feather. Broken but not quite beautiful.

Movement.

Light flickers.

Not in the upstairs windows, but in the basement. I see it from the squat windows peeking above the tilled flower beds. See it through the heavy curtains.

I hear it.

The hiss of electricity.

The hiss of serpents.

But this time, they don't scare me. Not really. In a twisted way, the sound makes me feel at home. Scared. Which is precisely where I belong.

The front door clicks open. Just an inch. Light flickers within. Inviting me in.

Calling me back.

Hissing whispers, beckoning. The ground slithers with them, snakes crawling over the grass, twisting over my shoes, but I don't fear them, not now.

I'm home.

I'm supposed to be home.

I take a step forward, toward the door that opens another inch, toward the snakes slithering over the doorframe.

A step home.

And a car of high schoolers drives past, honking

the horn and blasting music, laughing out the windows, and the darkness is gone, and the snakes are gone, and I am standing on the other side of the street staring at the closed front door of the house I tried so hard to escape.

I shudder hard.

Why am I back here?

Why did I come here?

I turn and hurry down the street.

As I round the corner, I swear I hear a voice from the house, faintly calling out my name.

I can't tell if it's my father or the clown.

I can't tell if there's a difference.

Andres

"Wow," I say as we step inside Caroline's house. "Your place is amazing!"

Caroline lives on the edge of town—which isn't that far, since our town is pretty small—in a huge house that looks like a museum. Maybe it's because I have so many brothers, but I don't think I've ever seen my place look this immaculate, no matter how many times my parents clean—or, as is often the case, force us to clean. Like, there are sculptures on the bookshelves and coffee table that I *know* would have been broken within an hour of being in my house. The first floor is open concept, with the kitchen open to the dining and living rooms, everything white and gray and perfect and lit by expensive-looking Edison-style lights and huge windows overlooking a yard filled with flower beds and trees.

"Thank you," Caroline says, blushing wildly. "Though it's not so fun on cleaning day."

We put our shoes in the entry hall and bring our bags to the basement den. Because of course this place has a basement den.

"Do you think he'll get here okay?" April asks as we head down the carpeted steps. Somehow, they've even managed to keep the *carpet* white and immaculate.

"Kyle?" I reply. "Of course."

I try to keep my voice assured, but in all honesty, I'm worried about him. It's taking all my self-control not to send a dozen texts asking where he is and if he needs a ride. We headed to each of our houses and then to the store before coming here, and we didn't see Kyle the entire time. Maybe he was taking some side streets. But in a town this size, where you see literally everyone everywhere all the time, it worries me.

I refuse to let the dark questions enter my mind, but they push at the edges.

What if the clown already took him? What if you'll never see him again?

The last makes my heart hurt, which is why I force it away.

The den is just as huge and clean as the rest of the house, with a few short windows in the upper corners and the biggest sectional sofa I've ever seen taking up three-quarters of the space. It curves around a coffee table covered in art books, and a TV the size of a small car is mounted to a wall, with a fireplace and a few gaming systems beneath.

"I figured we could sleep down here tonight," she says. "There should be enough room for three or so on the sofa, and we have air beds we can bring out—I'll move the coffee table out of the way. The bathroom is in there"—she points to the only other door down here—"and, yeah. Make yourselves at home."

Deshaun and April and I share a glance. We've all been to each other's houses, and not one of us lives anywhere nearly as nice as this. We stand there awkwardly, holding our bags of clothes and candy. But then I shrug and smile and head over to the sofa, flopping down and dropping my backpack to the floor, then dumping the grocery bag of candy across the coffee table.

The spell breaks, and the rest of my friends start settling in.

"Dad said he'd be home in an hour or so," Caroline says. "Is everyone okay with taco night?"

"Totally!" Deshaun says, stretching out on the sofa and poking April in the side, making her jump. She swats at him and giggles.

For a split second I can almost pretend that everything is how it was a year ago. Before we started going our separate ways, when we spent almost every waking moment together as a group. But the moment I think that, the space beside me feels emptier—this is where Kyle should be, but he's out there on his own.

Out there alone.

At least, I hope he's alone.

I pull out my phone and text him while the others head back upstairs to grab some snack food.

Kyle responds to my text fairly quickly. *On my way. There in five.*

I sigh and flop back on the sofa.

And keep sinking.

"Wh-what?" I stutter.

I try to sit up, but that movement makes me sink deeper.

I reach down to press myself up. My hand pushes *through* the leather of the sofa.

It's no longer leather.

It's quicksand.

I yelp and struggle to sit up, but the more I move, the faster the quicksand sucks me down. It squishes against me, reaches up past my chest. I struggle harder. Sink deeper. The sand presses all around me. Squeezes the air out of my lungs.

And above me, on the white ceiling, a million tiny black stars appear.

No, not stars.

Spiders.

Scuttling

down

the walls.

Swarming me.

I can hear their little feet, the clicking of their pincers as they draw near, heading toward my face and hands, the only parts of me left above the quicksand.

They're going to attack me. I squeeze my eyes and mouth shut. I ready for their little prickly legs, the sharp bite of their pincers. I want to scream, but I know if I do, they'll crawl down my throat.

Something hard smacks me on the forehead.

I gasp and look up, jolting upright.

I can sit upright.

April and the others are standing at the foot of the stairs. Deshaun has a handful of candy—he chucked a candy bar at my head.

"Yo, dude," he says. "You okay? You look like you zoned out for a minute."

"Quicksand," I gasp. I push myself to stand. My heart races so fast I feel like I ran a mile in gym. I don't think I'll be able to sleep on that sofa. I don't know if I'll be able to sleep ever again.

"Quicksand?" April asks. She takes one step toward me.

"And spiders."

That stops her. She *hates* spiders. She looks around wildly, as if expecting them to leap from the shadows at her. But the spiders—just like the quicksand—are gone.

"What?" Deshaun whispers. "You saw both? At the same time?"

"But that's impossible," April says.

Caroline shakes her head.

"No, don't you see? Now that it's stronger, it can show us anything to scare us. It can use anyone's fear." She looks from April to Deshaun and then to me. "It's gotten smarter. We can't know what to expect anymore. None of us are safe."

"But it's all just in our heads, right?" Deshaun asks.

Right. Caroline hadn't told him where she'd gotten the scratch on her face. She opens her mouth to speak, but before she can, I feel something under my fingernails.

"I don't think so," I whisper, pulling out a few grains of sand. Deshaun steps forward and peers at the sand on my fingertip.

"No way," he whispers. April and Caroline crowd in behind him, but right as they near, right as he reaches for the granules, the sand disappears.

"It can make things real now," Deshaun whispers. He swallows hard and looks up at me.

And no matter how many times he's said it, no

matter how much we've all tried to convince ourselves to just *be strong, don't let fear get to you*, I can
see it in his eyes.

He's terrified.

Caroline

Even though I faced my own nightmares in my bed-room years ago, it feels different to know the clown has made its way into my house to attack others. Different knowing that this time, it can leave a trace. It feels worse.

We aren't safe here.

We aren't safe anywhere.

We sit there for a few minutes, trying to formulate some sort of plan. But there is no plan. Last time, the clown only attacked us when we were alone and vulnerable. Last time, it only showed us what we were personally afraid of. Last time, it didn't leave a trace.

Last time, we had a chance of standing up to it and winning.

The doorbell rings and I jump.

"Kyle," Andres says.

"I'll get it," I respond. "I was going to start making cider, anyway."

As I walk up the steps, a clinging sadness hits me. Like when I glance over my shoulder, that will be the last time I see my friends again. I know that's not true. It can't be true.

But right now, all things feel possible. I don't want to let any of my friends out of my sight.

I'm scared of what will happen when I do.

I make my way to the front door. The doorbell rings right as I reach out toward the doorknob.

I freeze. My hands hover an inch from the handle.

Something feels off.

Something feels wrong.

Outside, I swear I hear the jingle of bells.

My heart lodged in my throat, I lean forward.

Toward the peephole.

To see who is outside.

To see my mother.

She stands there in the dress we buried her in, dirt caking her skin, clumps of earth and vines tangled in her hair, her skin mottled and peeling and gray.

"Let me in, Sunnybunny," she says in her silky voice. "I've missed you so much. I just want to hold you close and never let go. Sunnybunny, are you there?"

Her eyes suddenly blaze blue. She leans forward, her burning blue eye going straight to the peephole. I yelp and jump back.

"I seeee yoouuuu," she calls in a singsong voice. Only it's not her voice anymore. It also sounds like the clown.

"Let me in, Sunnybunny!" she calls out. Her fist slams against the door. I take a step back.

She pounds again on the door, making the frame rattle. "LET ME IN!" she howls. She slams the door with every word. "LET! ME! IN! LET! ME! IN!"

Tears fill my eyes and I stumble backward and the whole wall is rattling, is shaking, is about to crash down.

"Please," I whisper. "Please go away."

The pounding stops.

Silence stretches, so deep I can hear the *thud thud thud* of my frantic heart.

"Caroliiiiiine," my mother sings. Her voice seems to shift outside, circling the house impossibly. "I'm coming for you, Sunnybunny. Mommy's been *so lonely.* Don't you want to join Mommy?" The voice pauses. Right behind me. I don't turn around, but I swear I smell the grave dirt on her. Swear I feel her breath on my neck. "After all," she growls, "my death is all. Your. Fault!"

Her hands slap down on my shoulders just as the doorbell rings again.

I scream and turn around.

But there's no one there. No one there.

The door opens and I scream a second time, whipping back around, but it's only Kyle.

He stares at me.

"Sorry," he says. "I didn't mean to barge in, but I've been ringing for a while, and then I heard a scream and—"

I cut him off, running toward him and wrapping my arms around him, because he's real, he's solid and warm and real, and before I know it, I'm sobbing on his shoulder and he's awkwardly putting his arms around me.

"It's okay," he whispers. "It's okay."

I sob harder.

Because it's not.

It's not.

Deshaun

There's a new rule: No one is allowed to be alone. Ever.

"That's going to make going to the bathroom a little awkward," Andres says, but April's glare knocks the humor out of him. "Just trying to lighten the mood," he mutters. Not that it works. The mood is anything but light.

The five of us stand in Caroline's kitchen. After Kyle came in and Caroline relayed what had happened to her, she didn't want to be alone up here. And honestly, the rest of us didn't want to be alone in Caroline's basement. Even if there were four of us and even if it was nicer than most of our actual living rooms, it was still a basement.

It was still underground,

difficult to escape. If we
had to escape. Not that I thought there *was* an escape.
I'd even brought a few protective amulets and crystals
from the house, but seeing that the clown could actually hurt people made all that feel like child's play.
Toys wouldn't hurt a monster that strong. Nothing
could.

"What do you think it wants?" I ask.

"To scare us," April says.

"It's doing a good job so far," Caroline replies.

April doesn't say anything, but I catch her biting
her lip in worry.

I know she feels guilty that she hasn't seen anything. I know she feels—somehow—like this is all
her fault. I know because I feel guilt as well. I've had
two years to plan and protect, and I've gotten lazy.
I'm no more prepared to fight this thing than I was
the first time.

"I never should have brought it up yesterday," I
hear April whisper. I put my arm over her shoulders.

"It isn't your fault," I say. Even though we all
know it's true, it doesn't make her feel any better.

Caroline has the TV on in the background,

playing some sitcom with a prerecorded laugh track. It's strange, the five of us standing there in near silence, with the TV laughing in the background at jokes we only half catch. Nothing seems funny right now. Nothing.

I look over to Kyle. He's the only one not in the kitchen. He sits on the sofa closest to the door leading to the back porch, staring outside, saying nothing. He hasn't said much since coming in. When April bravely asked if he'd seen anything on his walk, he shook his head. But I know how his shoulders hang when he's lying.

I wish I could get him away to ask him what's wrong, but that would break the number one rule. We have to stick together. Have to. I know that if I were to push Kyle, he'd leave.

I feel worst for Andres; he's tried comforting Kyle a number of times, but Kyle is being a jerk and ignoring him. I can tell it hurts Andres's feelings, and I know that's why Andres keeps trying to be funny. I don't know if I want to give Kyle a hug and tell him it's going to be okay or punch him in the shoulder for being so mean. I can't forget what he said at lunch, can't forget how angry he looked.

I wasn't just saying it earlier; he reminded me of his father. At least, of what I'd heard about his father. I'd only seen his dad once, in passing, but even that had been enough to creep me out. I can't believe Kyle was able to last as long in that house as he did.

"Here," Caroline says, handing me a mug.

I jolt in surprise; I've been so in my head I haven't even noticed her ladling out the mugs of steaming spiced cider.

"Thanks," I reply.

She smiles in response and goes over to give Kyle his. He takes it and holds it in his hands, still staring out the window.

"To us," Caroline says when she's returned with her own mug. "To a friendship that will last forever."

"To friendship," April replies. We all raise our mugs and clink. All except Kyle, who drinks his without looking at us.

April glances over at him, her face concerned.

"Don't worry," I whisper, hoping he can't hear over the laugh track of the TV. "He'll be okay."

The laughing on the TV grows louder.

For some reason, chills race over my skin. I turn and face the television.

The characters on the sitcom all sit in a living room on their sofas. But they're no longer talking to each other. They're staring at us. Laughing.

"They think they're safe," says one of the TV characters. More laughter erupts from the speakers, so loud it hurts my ears.

"They think they can stop me," says another.

More laughter.

"They think that I can't hurt them," says a third.

Uproarious laughter, so loud it makes the sculptures rattle on their pedestals.

"But I can," they say in unison. "I can hurt them whenever I want to now."

More laughter. One of the sculptures beside me topples over, an intricate glass piece, shattering all over the ground. Glass explodes around me.

As one, the five of us jump and yelp out in fear.

The TV turns to static.

I look down, panting, to see two thin lines across my arm begin to bleed, from where the glass shot out and scratched me.

"Deshaun!" April yells, grabbing hold of my arm. Caroline is there in a heartbeat with a clean towel.

Seconds later, everyone is there, crowding around me, making sure I'm okay.

Adrenaline courses through my veins, so strong I can't feel a thing. It feels like a dream. A very, very bad dream.

"You all saw that," I say. It isn't a question.

Caroline looks up from bandaging my arm with gauze. The wounds aren't too deep. It's okay. We're okay. For now.

Caroline nods.

So does Andres. And even Kyle, who stares at my arm with a haunted expression on his face. The only person who doesn't nod is April, and she looks horribly lost and horribly afraid because of it.

Kyle

I shouldn't be here.
    I shouldn't be here.
    I shouldn't be here.

Andres

Caroline's dad—who refuses to be called anything but Tim—gets home half an hour after the TV incident. If he notices the broken sculpture, he doesn't mention it. We've done a good job of cleaning it up, and Deshaun is all bandaged and fine.

The only thing that Tim *does* comment on is how quiet it is in the house.

"Don't you want the TV on or something?" he asks.

We all shout no in unison, and April hastily scrambles together a lie about how it was because we'd taken a vow not to watch TV all weekend and read instead, as part of a school challenge.

Nice one, I mouth to her. She smiles a little, but it slips instantly.

Thankfully, Caroline's dad (it's really hard calling him Tim; it's always weird when adults ask you to call them by their first names) immediately gets to work on dinner, and the house is soon filled with the sounds of sizzling veggies and meat.

While we wait, he sets out a heaping plate of loaded nachos. It takes all my self-control not to gorge myself on those alone. I have to keep reminding myself there are still tacos. And ice cream. And all that discount Halloween candy. I don't know how I can be so hungry—maybe being scared for my life makes me feel starved.

Kyle, however, barely takes a bite.

Every time I look over to him, my heart aches. I want to go sit by him and tell him it's going to be okay. I want to be there for him, like Deshaun is for April. They stand next to each other at the kitchen counter, idly talking to Caroline and her dad about school. Every once in a while, Deshaun leans into April, a gentle nudge, like an unconscious reminder that they are there. Together. For each other.

Kyle sulks on the other side of the kitchen, a

plate of maybe three nachos in his hand and a sort of mechanical expression on his face as he nods along to the conversation without even listening. I go stand next to him, but he doesn't even seem to realize I exist. When I put a hand on his shoulder, he actually shakes it off.

Fine, then, I think, and head back to stand by the others. They at least include me in the conversation.

When they're done, we help ourselves to tacos. I'm grateful that Tim doesn't force us to have an awkward sit-down family-style meal. Instead, we all stand around or sit at various tables, eating and trying to keep up the strained conversation. I keep thinking about what happens after this; somehow, we have to convince Kyle to go to the graveyard to find Jeremy and the others. A part of me almost feels guilty, like it's my fault they went missing.

Maybe if we'd stayed at the carnival longer, we could have prevented them from getting tricked by the clown.

Maybe if we had actually stuck together, none of this would be happening.

"How was the carnival?" Tim asks.

I nearly choke on my taco.

"It was fun," Caroline says. She glances at April. "We were actually planning on going back tonight."

Kyle jolts and looks up at the group. Finally back to Earth.

"We were?" he asks.

"Yeah," April says. She doesn't make eye contact when she speaks. Instead, she looks at me, trying to convey the secret message, and even though this is news to me, it finally clicks—this is the cover we're telling Caroline's dad so we can leave and check out the graveyard later. I wonder if they plan on telling Kyle the truth, or if they're going to keep this from him as well. "We were talking about it when you ran back to your place."

"I—" Kyle begins.

"Come on," Deshaun says. "It'll be fun."

Kyle mumbles something I can't hear and looks back to his plate. I don't know if it's him agreeing or not. I also know he doesn't really have a choice if we all leave. It's not like he'd be so grumpy he'd opt to stay here alone. Right?

While Caroline and the others clean up the plates, I offer to take out the garbage. I roll the garbage can to the curb and head back toward the open garage.

Halfway there, I get the distinct feeling I'm being watched, and I pause.

"Have you missed me, Andres?" comes the clown's voice.

I turn around and look toward the street.

The clown stands in the middle of the road, its eyes blackened by diamonds of ink and its face a wicked sneer. It towers at least ten feet tall, its clothing tattered. It looks skeletal, demonic, and more terrifying than ever before.

It takes a step forward. The concrete under its feet cracks.

"Because I've missed you. I've missed all of you. Now we can play together. Now I can bring *all* my friends."

"You . . . y-y-you're not real," I stammer. I try to take a step backward, toward the house, but my feet don't move. "We've defeated you once. We're going to do it again."

The clown tilts its head to the side.

"Is that what you think?" it asks. Its smile widens. Black tar drips from its teeth. "I'm stronger than ever before, Andres. All because of you. All because you left your friends to me. Their fears were so tasty. And now that I have fed, I can do things you've never dreamed of." It takes another step forward. "When we are done playing, I'll make you *wish* you were dead!"

The clown raises its arms, then explodes into a swarm of bats and rats.

Instantly, the suburban landscape bursts into flames. The heat sears my face but I can't move my feet. I'm frozen, staring at the apocalyptic destruction, my breathing so hard and fast it burns worse than the smoldering air.

From the burning wreckage, blackened skeletons begin to shuffle out, moaning, burning, shambling toward me, as the sky fills with screeching bats and wailing ghosts, plague rats flood the street, and spiders the size of dogs creep from behind cars.

The rats and spiders scuttle closer. Up the driveway. Toward me. Toward the garage.

I finally kick into gear, jumping back and slamming the door to the house so loud the floor shakes.

But not before a giant rat scuttles over the threshold and into the house.

It races across the kitchen and disappears behind the garbage can.

"What was that?" Caroline's dad yelps. He immediately runs over to the garbage can and nudges it aside with his foot, holding a rolling pin like a weapon.

There's nothing behind the garbage can.

"What was that?" he repeats to me, his eyes wide. Everyone else is staring at Tim and me with terrified looks on their faces. "Was that a rat? That was *way* too big to be a rat. Did you see a rat come in?"

His voice is frantic, and I can't answer.

"Where did it go?" Tim asks. "I'm sure I saw it."

"Maybe it was just a shadow, Daddy," Caroline says consolingly. I catch the tremble in her voice. "Or a leaf."

Tim pushes the garbage can farther. But the rat isn't there, and there's nowhere it could have gone.

He looks at me, breathing deep.

"I *hate* rats," he admits.

I swallow the bile rising in the back of my throat.

He's afraid of rats.

He was able to see what the clown created.

I look to my friends.

In the past, it was just us who could see the clown and its monstrous creations. I had always assumed it was only able to target kids. Now an adult has seen something. An adult who has—to our knowledge—never encountered the clown before. Does that mean that Caroline's dad is also a victim? Or does it mean something more sinister? Something more dire?

Maybe the clown's nightmares are no longer confined to the five of us, the ones who've seen it, the ones it's actively hunting.

Maybe now everyone's at risk.

April

This can't be real. This can't be happening.

Caroline's dad scours the house, looking for the rat that we all know isn't there. At least, not anymore.

We excuse ourselves to the basement. We tell him we want to stay out of his hair while he searches.

The truth is, we need to talk. Now.

"What's going on?" I demand the moment we're all downstairs. "Did Caroline's dad just see what I think he saw?"

Andres nods slowly. His face is ashen.

"That's not possible," Deshaun says. He's trying to keep his voice calm and rational, which is what he does when he's terrified but doesn't want to show it.

"Then how do you explain it?" Andres asks. "The clown appeared in the street and said that it could do things we'd never dreamed of. Everything went crazy, and then . . ." He shudders, clearly suppressing the rest of what happened. "And then I slammed the door right as a rat came in. Your dad saw it, Caroline. The clown was able to reach him."

"But how? My dad's never mentioned the clown. And he's, well, he's an *adult*."

Andres shakes his head slowly, disbelief clear on his face. Up until now, we had just sort of assumed that the clown was only after kids. I mean, it had appeared to *us*. But maybe we had just taken it for granted. Like the thought that the clown was actually gone.

"Isn't it obvious?" Andres asks. "The clown's just showing off now. It's fed. It has more power than it ever did before. It can make nightmares manifest for anyone. Maybe even the whole town."

My gut sinks at the thought. The whole town might be in trouble.

But if Caroline's dad was able to see the rat, why haven't I seen anything yet?

Before I can say anything, Kyle stands up.

"I thought we promised we weren't going to talk about this," he growls.

"We did, but—" I begin.

"So now you think it's okay to just break promises? Is that what being friends means to you?"

"That's not what's going on at all," Deshaun says, his voice still calm. "Things have changed. This is getting more dangerous than we could have imagined. Everyone could be at risk. We have no idea what the clown—"

"Enough about the stupid clown!" Kyle yells. "I'm sick of this. There is no clown. There was no rat. You all are just hallucinating because April got this stupid idea stuck in your heads." He points at my chest. It feels like getting punched in the gut.

"We're telling the truth," I say. "The clown . . ."

Kyle steps up to me. And maybe it's my imagination, but I swear I see a flash of blue in his eyes. My words stop in my throat.

"Have you seen the clown?" he asks softly. "Tell me the truth, April. Have you seen the clown for yourself? Or anything out of the ordinary beyond that note that may or may not have been left in your drawer as a prank—if you're telling the truth about not leaving it yourself?"

My mouth drops open.

Words are knotted in my chest and my breath burns and I feel my face flush because the truth is, *no*, I haven't seen anything. Just the note.

"Exactly," he says, taking my silence for confirmation. He stands and looks to everyone. "You're all just letting this go to your heads. The clown isn't back. It's gone. Dead. Buried."

"But Jeremy and the others—"

"Probably just ran away," Kyle says, interrupting Deshaun. "Or maybe they joined the carnival. Kids play pranks like that all the time." He looks at me. "Isn't that right, April?"

"I—"

"This is all just a prank of yours. Because you felt bad that we were all growing apart. Well, reality check, that's just what happens. We grow up. We grow apart. It's not like we ever had anything in common anyway, just that stupid clown. And guess what. The clown is gone. And so is our only reason for hanging out."

He stomps over and grabs his bag.

"Where are you going?" Andres asks, standing as if to intercept him.

"Home," Kyle growls. "Away from all of this nonsense." He glowers at Andres. "I know she's your friend, but I would have thought that you of all people would have had my back."

Before any of us can say anything, he thunders up the stairs.

Andres steps forward, but Deshaun reaches out and holds him back as we hear the door slam upstairs.

"Let him go," Deshaun says sadly. "He needs some time to cool off."

We stand in silence, staring at the space Kyle just occupied.

Letting him go feels wrong. So wrong. The clown is out there. The clown has clearly already gotten to him. I hate to think what other horrors the clown might have in store for him, especially if he's out on his own. But Deshaun knows him better than any of us do—even Andres—and if he says we should let him go, we'll listen.

Deshaun comes over and takes my hand. It's only when he does so that I realize I'm shaking.

"It's okay," he says soothingly. "He didn't mean those things."

"He did," I reply. "What if he's right? What if this *is* all just our imaginations or something?"

"I know what I saw," Andres says. "*And* felt. I've already been buried in quicksand and attacked by spiders. I don't even want to think about what might come next."

"And I've seen zombies," says Caroline. She touches her cheek, where the faintest impression of a scratch still lingers. "They were real."

"And I've seen the clown itself," Deshaun finishes. "There's no way it's just our imaginations. Jeremy and the others are missing, and we have every reason to believe the clown took them. They need our help. Heck, if the clown is powerful enough to make even Caroline's dad see something, the whole town needs our help."

"But what do we do?" I ask. Tears form in my eyes, and I feel like I'm just repeating myself, but I still can't find a way around it. "We only defeated the clown when we were together. And even then it didn't last."

Deshaun nods.

"We had already planned on going to the grave-yard," he says. "I think that's the best option. Maybe there are more clues there. Or maybe we can drop by the carnival and ask around—I'm sure someone must have seen something."

"But what about Kyle?" Andres asks. "We can't just leave him out there by himself. Who knows what will happen?"

"I know," Deshaun says. He looks to his feet. "But I think if we follow, he'll just push us away more. My parents are home; they'll watch after him."

I know him well enough to know when he's lying; he's more worried about Kyle than he wants us to believe. Kyle is basically his brother. I know Deshaun feels responsible for him.

"Look at it this way," Deshaun continues, and I think he might just be explaining it aloud to himself, hoping it will make him feel better. "We know we need to stick together, and right now, we need hard evidence to prove to Kyle that this is really happening. He's scared, but he's not stupid. If we bring him something he can't deny is real, we might have a chance."

"But what if there isn't any evidence?" I ask.

"Either way, we'll know. But if there's one thing I've learned about the clown, it's that it is far from discreet. It *wants* to be seen. It wants us to be scared."

He's right. The clown gets its strength from making us scared, from showing us our deepest nightmares. It doesn't want to hide.

Which begs the question . . . why hasn't it shown itself to me?

Kyle

I can't believe them.

I trusted them.

I *trusted* them.

But they won't shut up about the stupid clown. They won't stop pretending it's back. I know it isn't back. Because I'm not going back. I'm not going—

> *I'm back.*

I stand outside my house. My old house. My real house?

It towers above me. The porch light is on.

The basement lights are on.

I pause on the other side of the street.

Pumpkins line the sidewalk leading to the porch,

lights flickering within. The ghost swaying in the breeze glows pale blue. I know the pumpkins weren't there before, and a small, distant part of me knows they shouldn't be there now, but the rest wants to believe my mom put them out. That she knew I'd be walking by. That this was her way of reaching out and letting me know she was okay. That it was okay: I could come home.

I cross the street.

Every step toward my house, and the air grows colder.

Every step toward my house, and I can make out the faces carved in the pumpkins.

Kids. The missing kids. My body shakes as I examine each one in turn, their intricate expressions pulling me even closer.

The first is Jeremy's little brother, looking at me with concern clear on his face.

Then the girl with pigtails and braces.

Then the twins.

Then Jeremy.

The moment I near, his face moves.

His mouth opens in a silent plea:

HELP!

The front door opens. Snakes slither down the steps, coil around my feet.

I look up.

I see my father, standing in the shadows and sharp lines of light.

My father, with glowing blue eyes.

My father, dressed as the clown.

Deshaun

"I still don't think we should let him wander alone," April says beside me. "It isn't safe."

I squeeze her hand. We're almost at the graveyard. If *anyone* doesn't feel safe right now, it's me. Us.

"Kyle will be fine," I say for the hundredth time. I'm definitely still trying to reassure myself. "I'll text my parents when we're back at Caroline's to make sure he got home okay."

"But what if he doesn't make it? What if the clown gets him?"

"It won't," Andres says. "Kyle's a lot tougher than we give him credit for. If the clown *does* try to get him, I'd be more worried about the clown."

"That's not funny," April whispers, so soft only I can hear it.

"He'll be fine," I repeat. "Promise."

We reach the cemetery. The night air feels like it dropped twenty degrees since we left Caroline's house. Our breath comes out in clouds, and the barren sky above seems to eat up heat. It's a sharp contrast to the blaring music and flashing lights of the carnival across the road. I stare up at the hills of the graveyard and try to calm myself. Chills race down my spine as images from years ago race through my thoughts.

Being trapped out here. Trying to escape and unable to flee. Being trapped in the graveyard, trying to run and hide from ghosts that wailed and screamed my name until the sun rose and I was finally able to leave. Something about tonight feels so similar to then.

The danger. The isolation.

And the presence. Even as we stand here, at the base of the hill, staring up at the stunted trees and tombstones, it feels like we are in forbidden territory. It feels like we are being watched. I keep searching for meandering skeletons or decaying ghouls or the telltale burning blue eyes of the clown. Or even a group of teenagers getting into trouble—after all, it's a weekend, the night after Halloween. Surely some-one is up here testing their bravery.

The cemetery is eerily empty. The lack of people is almost a presence in itself.

"Are you sure about this?" Andres asks me. He shudders. "You didn't see what I saw earlier. This place . . . this isn't right."

"I'm sure," I reply. "We need to find proof that Jeremy and the others were here. More proof than the hat, which Kyle never got to see," I finish. "It's the only way to convince Kyle. And even if we don't convince him, hopefully we can find a trace of Jeremy. Hopefully we can find a way to help. They need us."

Andres grunts. "Fine. If you say so. But this is my good deed for the next twenty years, got it?"

I grin slightly and hug April, who stands there with her arms crossed over her chest and a very unhappy look on her face. Caroline is the only one who seems at all prepared for this. She brought a backpack filled with flashlights and small spades, and she carries a metal baseball bat. Just in case. Her face is set in determination.

"Come on," she says. She trudges up the hill. We follow.

It doesn't take long to find the grave. There's a tug in my gut that pulls me forward, a fear that intensifies even as it intoxicates.

I feel like I could close my eyes and walk and I'd arrive here. No matter where I started. No matter where I wanted to go. This place would draw me back.

The tombstone stands below a gnarled tree. Its surface is worn smooth and weathered, and just like before, there are words painted in black on the surface:

HERE LIE THE BODIES OF
FIVE NAUGHTY CHILDREN
BUT THERE'S ROOM FOR FIVE MORE

My stomach twists in fear and nausea. The dirt at the base of the tombstone is a freshly churned mound. And at its side are five shovels. Caroline steps over to the shovels and looks at them. There's writing on the handles.

"Don't touch them," April warns as Caroline's hand goes to one. "It could be a trap."

Caroline drops her hand and instead shines the light over the five shovels.

"It wants us to dig," Caroline says, her voice a mix of disgust and wonder. "It wants us to dig our own graves. It's even given us shovels with our names on them."

"That's twisted," Andres says. "Why would we want to dig our own graves?"

"Because," comes a terribly familiar voice from behind the tombstone, "soon you will be *begging* to be buried here."

I stumble back as two enormous satin-gloved hands clamp on top of the tombstone.

"What is it?" April asks. But I barely hear her. None of us do. Caroline and Andres and I can only stare up in horror as the clown presses itself up to standing.

If I thought it was terrifying before, it was nothing compared with the monster before us now.

The clown is barely human. Its face is chalk white and skeletal, its cheeks caved in to the bone and its skin pulled so tight I can see the black gums in its mouth, its razor-sharp teeth grinding in a grin that splits its face in half. Red paint frames its blackened lips, and its white ears poke out of its bushy red hair like bat wings. Its eyes blaze fierce blue from within black diamonds that look burned into its skin.

As it stretches up, reaching higher and higher, talons shred from its gloves, and its floppy red shoes split as its feet elongate and grow claws. When it smiles down at us, saliva drips from its wolflike teeth.

"How do you like me now that I've fed, children?" the clown asks, cackling. Caroline and Andres and I can't move, can't speak. Only April is able to move, and she looks between the three of us and toward the grave with fear on her face. "This is only the beginning," the clown continues. "You thought you had destroyed me, but you were wrong. I was merely waiting. Growing stronger. You hurt me." Its slashed grin turns into a frown that is somehow even more terrifying. Its voice goes singsong. "You hurt my feelings. And I had to lie underground for two years, and you know what I did? I thought of all the horrible things I would do to you when I was free. And here I am. I could take all four of you right now, but that wouldn't be so fun, would it? I want you to beg for me to stop. I want you to wish you were buried in the same place you buried me. Then maybe I will stop. Maybe."

The frown snaps back to a smile. When it speaks again, I know its words are echoing in my head alone.

"I hope you are ready to be afraid, Deshaun. You thought you knew fear before. But you were so, so wrong."

It leans over, stretches its face so it is only a foot from mine, its blue eyes burning so bright I can't see anything else.

"You think you can help the others. But you are wrong. You won't even be able to help yourself. Not where you're going. You always thought you were so smart, didn't you? Top of your class? So prepared for my return. You thought of *everything*. Well, let's see if you can think your way out of this one."

Its blue eyes are bright. So bright.

Distantly, I hear someone screaming. Feel someone shaking me.

But the blue pulls me forward.

Into the brightness.

Into the dark.

April

I can't see a thing.

Nothing is happening except Deshaun and Caroline and Andres look like they see a ghost but all I see is the tombstone and the tree and then Andres starts screaming. He screams and turns and runs down the hill before I can call out to him, but then Caroline starts screaming as well. She flees in the other direction.

And then something happens to Deshaun.

He steps forward. His eyes open. His face slackens.

Entranced.

I shake his arm. Try to get him to come to his senses.

He steps forward, and the moment his foot touches the mound of freshly turned grave dirt, he starts to fade.

His arm slips from my grasp. I try to catch it again, but it's like my hand is passing through smoke. I can't get him. Can't reach him. Can't help as he disappears from view.

Then it's my turn to scream.

Andres

I run at full speed from the spiders that scuttle from the clown's mouth and the rats crawling out from under its pant legs. They swarm behind me, the rats with blazing blue eyes and gnashing teeth, the spiders growing with every step, until they are the size of cats, of dogs, of small cars. I stumble over tombstones. Squelch through quicksand. Fear is a blind, frantic pulse inside me. I don't know where I'm going. I don't know where the others are.

I stopped thinking of them the moment the clown leaned over and told me it would eat my family for breakfast and I saw that first spider leg poking from between its teeth.

Maybe I'm running home. I hope that's where my feet are taking me as I careen down the hill. Spiders the size of cars keep pace with me, their long legs piercing the soft earth, their pincers dripping green acid and their beady eyes glowing like blue-white moons.

Ahead of me, behind me, I hear screaming. April's. Caroline's.

My brothers'.

I look up from where I'm running just for a second. Just in time to see my brothers in the valley below me. Standing beside a tombstone.

The clown, monstrous and tall, standing behind them.

The clown waves at me. My brothers scream out.

The clown's mouth opens wide, cracks, and splits its face.

And as I scream and stumble, as the spiders and rats scuttle behind me, laughing at my fear, the clown snaps down at the waist and devours my brothers whole.

Caroline

I run straight down the hill, straight toward my house, as the ghost of my mother howls behind me, screaming such terrible things. I slam my hands to my ears. But it doesn't help. I can still hear her. Can still hear her saying it is my fault. That she got sick because of me. That if I had tried a little harder, I could have helped her. I could have made her better. But I didn't. I didn't.

She yells that this too is all my fault. *I* was the one who goaded my friends into unearthing the clown.

I was the one who started this whole nightmare.

The worst part is, I know she is right. On this,

she's right. If I hadn't made fun of them, if I hadn't poked them, we might have left the graveyard that night two years ago without ever digging up the grave, without ever pulling out that cursed tin box. If I hadn't been a bully, everyone would be safe. If I hadn't been mean—as mean as the clown—nothing bad would have happened.

If not for me, Jeremy and the others might still be alive.

If not for me, my mother might still be alive too.

Guilt burns inside me, and as I run, a new sound fills my ears. Thunder.

Rumbling shakes the ground. An earthquake?

No.

Barking.

I glance over my shoulder, and rather than the ghoulish ghost of my mother, there are dogs scrambling up from the dirt, unearthing themselves and shaking off the wet soil. But in that one glance I know they aren't normal dogs—their eyes blaze blue, and their teeth stick out of foaming mouths like saber-toothed tigers, and I can see ribs and bones through the scraggly fur of a few of them.

Zombie dogs.

They howl when they spot me. And then they take off down the hill.

I focus all my attention on running even as the dogs run faster, gaining on me, their paws smacking the earth and making it rumble and shake. I lose my footing. Scramble back up. Run harder. Faster. Even as a small voice inside me says I shouldn't run. I'm not worth saving.

This is all my fault.

Tears fill my eyes and spill down my cheeks. Breath burns like fire in my lungs.

I see an empty car parked ahead of me on the street.

I lean in, run full speed.

And when I reach the car I pray it's unlocked, jerk open the door, and slam it shut. I lock the door and close my eyes, curling up into a tight little ball in the driver's seat and squeezing my hands to my ears, my eyes to my knees, rocking back and forth as seconds later thunder rolls over the car, making it shudder as the dogs slam against the sides, beating on the windows, biting at the door handles, trying to get in.

"Go away," I whisper, frantic, rocking back and forth and trying to block out the noise. "Go away, please go away, please go away."

"Let me in, Caroline," comes the clown's sneering voice. Comes my mom's cajoling voice. Comes both of their voices at once. "I only want to play with you. Let me in, Sunnybunny. Let me in!"

"Caroline, let me in, please!"

I blink my eyes open.

Andres stands outside the passenger door, slamming on the glass, his eyes wide with fright.

Nothing else out there.

But he looks like he's running from something horrible.

I unlock the door and he jumps in, slamming the door shut and locking it behind him.

He collapses back into the seat.

"Did you see that?" he asks through his gasping breaths. "Did you *see* it?!"

I nod, speechless. But I don't know what he saw. It doesn't matter. No matter what, we know it was horrible.

"Where are the others?" he asks, looking into the back seat. "Didn't they follow you?"

"No," I'm finally able to gasp. "I thought they followed *you*?"

We both stare up the hill.

Toward the tombstone where we left April and Deshaun.

From here, we can't see anything. No monsters running down the hillside. No April or Deshaun.

"Do you think we should go up there?" Andres asks after a moment.

Lights from the carnival flicker over the hills, making the tombstones cast harsh shadows. Those shadows could be hiding anything. The only sound is the carnival music: cheerful, menacing. A reminder that even though there are people nearby, we are alone in our fear.

I can't answer. I know I should say yes. I know we should go help April and Deshaun. They need us.

But fear has me rooted. Along with my mother's words: *This is your fault, this is your fault.*

I know it's true.

I know it's all true.

And I'm too scared to do anything about it.

Kyle

"Come inside, Kyle," my father says. His eyes burn blue. His clown costume flickers. *He* flickers. Now my dad, now the clown, now the same person. Maybe they were always the same person. "Come back home."

Snakes slither over his feet, tangle down the porch steps, twine around my ankles.

I am terrified. But I am also past the fear.

I deserve the fear.

I deserve to be home.

My father opens the door wide.

"Come inside," the clown repeats. "You can't run away from who you are forever."

More snakes tumble out the front door. Their

hissing grows louder. The sound fills my head, makes it impossible to question. He's right. He's right.

This is who I am. This is where I'm meant to be.

I take a step forward.

The snakes part with every step.

Making way for me. A path of poison.

Bringing me back to where I belong.

April

I stumble to my knees as Deshaun disappears completely. One moment he's there, the faintest wisp of a figure. The next, he's gone.

"Deshaun!" I scream out for the millionth time.

But he isn't there. *He isn't there*. I fumble around in the dirt, reaching out for the legs or fingertips that I know I won't touch again.

Tears fall to the overturned earth, to my trembling hands. I can't bring myself to stand. I can't get my legs to work. Can't get *reality* to work.

Deshaun is gone.

But he can't be gone.

"*Deshaun!*" I yell, and all I can think is how

awful I've been to him lately, how distant, how distracted. I've been a horrible girlfriend and now he's gone, *gone*, and I have to get him back.

The thought fills me with resolve, a dull ache. I push myself to stand. My legs shake and wobble, but I don't collapse.

And that's when I realize that Deshaun isn't the only one missing.

Andres and Caroline are nowhere to be seen.

I run to the edge of the hill and look deeper into the graveyard. Nothing. I circle the top of the hill, but I don't see anyone among the shadowed tombstones. No sign of Deshaun or Andres or Caroline. Just the graveyard to one side and the carnival to the other.

I make my way back over to the spray-painted tombstone and kick the shovels. They clatter loudly, loud enough to wake the dead. That's what I'm hoping for. That's what I want.

"Where are you?" I scream. It's only as I call out that I feel it—the anger. The rage. Not at my friends, no.

At the clown.

The clown who still hasn't shown its face to me.

The clown who has scared or tricked or taken all my friends from me.

"Why are you hiding from me?" I yell. I turn on the spot, staring out at the empty, moonlit graveyard. Nothing rustles. Nothing stirs. Even the wind is quiet. "Are you scared of me? Is that it?"

Nothing responds.

Something wavers in my vision, but it's just another tear forming and falling.

"Why?" I ask, a whisper this time. "Why are you doing this to me?"

No response.

I look to the freshly churned earth at the base of the tombstone. An idea forms in my head.

Last time, there was a tunnel here. Maybe it's still there. Maybe Deshaun was taken down below. Maybe he's safe there. There, with the missing kids. Waiting for me. Caroline thought the shovels were so we could dig our own graves. Maybe I can use the clown's cruel tricks against it.

I grab a shovel; it has Kyle's name written on it.

I start to dig.

I don't know how long I hunch there, my arms and back aching, tears of fear and rage still dripping down into the soil. I dig until my arms shake so hard I can barely get them to move, but I keep going, even though the pile of dirt beside me barely seems to increase, nor does the hole I dig in the soft soil. I imagine Deshaun trapped in the caves below there, scared for his life, waiting for me. The thought gives me purpose, gives me hope. But it doesn't give me much more strength. I keep going, though, my movements getting slower and more strained with every shovelful of dirt I toss to the side. Tears continue to streak down my face.

I can't give up.

"April?"

I jolt upright and spin around, nearly smacking the intruder with the shovel in self-defense.

But it's only Andres. Andres and Caroline.

I gasp in relief and toss the shovel to the side, falling headfirst into Andres's arms. He squeezes me tight for the longest time. I sob onto his shoulder, unable to move or speak for what feels like hours. Caroline is there, rubbing my back. Eventually she breaks the spell of silence.

"What's going on up here?" Caroline asks. "Where is Deshaun? And what happened to your hands?"

I stand upright, and she gently takes my hands in hers to show me my palms. They're blistered and red and streaked with blood and tiny splinters. I hadn't even noticed it before, and even now my hands are just a dull throb. The moment I see the splinters, though, I wince.

"We should get you bandaged up," Andres says.

"I have a first-aid kit at home," Caroline replies. She looks at me. "Are you okay to walk?"

I shake my head. "I can't leave," I say. "I can't leave him."

"Who?"

Tears well in my eyes again.

"Deshaun. The clown took him. He just . . . he just . . ." I start crying again. Andres hugs me, trying to comfort me. I close my eyes and wish I could close out the pain, the truth. Deshaun is gone, and there's nothing we can do to save him. Just like Kyle. Just like Jeremy and the others.

The clown has taken everyone from me. And soon, I know, Caroline and Andres will be next.

Andres rocks me back and forth. After a few more frantic sobs, I manage to calm myself down a little bit.

"Tell us what happened," he says coolly and calmly. "What happened to Deshaun?"

I tell them. Choking on the words.

"We'll find him," Caroline says. "The clown's just playing with us. It doesn't . . . it doesn't want us dead yet. It wants revenge for what we did to it, and that means making us suffer."

"It's so horrible," I whisper. "Where did it take him? Where's Deshaun?"

"I don't know where Deshaun is," Andres admits. "But I'm sure he's okay. Deshaun's a smart kid. Smarter than all of us combined. You know that. He can take care of himself."

"But what if he's under there?" I ask, nodding to the pitiful pit I dug in front of the tombstone. "What if he needs us? We have to keep digging, just in case. I'm nearly there, I know it. I know—"

But before I can finish the sentence, the pile of dirt I built beside the pit shifts and slides. We watch in stunned horror as the pit fills itself, sucking down the shovels with it. Seconds later, it's a smooth mound again, as if I'd never been here. As if Deshaun no longer exists.

"I don't think he's under there," Andres says. Then his face brightens. "Let me try something."

He reaches into his pocket and pulls out his phone. I watch his screen. He dials Deshaun's number and puts it on speaker.

Deshaun's number rings and the tone from Andres's phone fills the silent graveyard. But I don't hear Deshaun's ringtone coming from anywhere. My heart drops. If he were here, if he were under the earth, surely we would hear it. Right?

Andres's phone rings forever.

And then, right when I think it's going to go to voicemail, Deshaun picks up.

"Hello?" he asks.

"Deshaun!" I yelp. I grab for Andres's phone. "Deshaun, what happened? Where are you?"

"I'm at home," he says. He sounds kind of confused. "Why would you ask? I told you that's where I was going."

"What?" I ask. "What do you mean? You just disappeared and—"

"I didn't disappear," he interrupts. "I told you, I got a text from Kyle saying he was back home and wanted to talk. So I came back here. Why are you freaking out? You said it was okay."

"But I—"

"Wait," Deshaun says. "Is this just another prank?"

"What do you mean?" I ask. My thoughts aren't connecting. This doesn't make sense. "You were here and you just vanished into thin air."

Deshaun laughs. But there's something wicked in the laughter, something angry. "I can't believe it—Kyle was right." He mutters something to someone in the room, and I hear Kyle respond, *She's losing it, man, I told you.*

"Listen," Deshaun continues, once more in that slow, calming tone that—right now—is infuriating. "I think we all just had too much candy tonight and our imaginations got the better of us. I left the graveyard after Andres and Caroline freaked and left us on top of the hill. I'm home now. Safe. Kyle's here too. I suggest you guys go back and have your sleepover and get the sugar out of your system. We can talk in the morning. When you've calmed down. All of you."

"Yeah, guys," comes Kyle's voice through the phone. "This is getting ridiculous. You're being childish. There's no clown. There's nothing strange going on except for whatever April's making up. Go to bed."

"Yeah," Deshaun says, taking the phone back. "I

think it's best if we just slept on it. I'll talk to you tomorrow."

There's a shuffle, as if Deshaun is setting down his phone. Did he forget to turn it off?

"I can't believe you started dating her," Kyle says distantly through the phone.

"Honestly, man, neither can I."

My blood goes cold. Before I can hear any more, Andres clicks off the phone. We all stare at each other. My heart thunders in my ears. My veins flood with betrayal. Tears form in my eyes, and I can't tell if they're from pain or anger or despair.

Their words echo in my head. The words I always feared they were saying when I wasn't around.

"April, I—" Andres begins.

I shake my head, pushing whatever he was going to say away.

"Forget them," I reply. "Let's just go home."

Before he or Caroline can try to stop me, I stomp down the hill, barely able to see where I'm going from the tears in my eyes.

My head swims with questions, my thoughts thick with sadness. How can I know what I saw anymore? That was Deshaun and Kyle. Safe at home. What if they were right? What if I *was* just losing it? What if I was making it all up, and everyone else was just hallucinating because I'd suggested it in the first place?

Don't they say that the simplest answer was usually the right one?

I know the truth:

The simplest answer isn't that the clown is back, hunting down my friends and messing with my head.

The simplest answer is that *I'm* making it all up. I'm hallucinating all of it. Both the clown, and the fact that my friends actually liked me. My friends were never my friends at all, and Deshaun never loved me.

And it's only when I reach the bottom of the hill that I realize it doesn't even really matter. Either the clown's back, or it's not—either way, I'm already living in my nightmare, and there's no way for me to change it.

Andres

"April," I say as we walk back to Caroline's house, "you know that wasn't really Deshaun, right?"

She doesn't respond. She stares out into the night sky, tears still streaming from her eyes and a dark expression on her face. I'm worried about her. I haven't seen her this upset since, well, since she and Caroline were enemies and Caroline insulted her for being overweight. It's a bone-deep sadness, one that I know nothing I say can cut through. Not that it stops me from trying.

"He wouldn't say that," I continue. "Neither of them would. Deshaun *loves* you. You're practically all he ever talks about."

Caroline *mhmm*s in agreement.

"I don't want to talk about it," April says.

"Okay," I say. I look to Caroline, who catches my eye and shrugs slightly. "Then we need to figure out what we're going to do. I still haven't gotten through to Kyle and—"

"What are you talking about?" April interrupts. "We just heard him on the phone."

"Yes, but—"

"Just because you don't want to believe it's him saying that mean stuff doesn't mean it isn't. He left you. Just like Deshaun left me."

Her words are a stab to the heart. Because deep down, I worry she's right. Hasn't that been my fear for the last few weeks? That Kyle was growing distant? That he was moving on? April keeps talking, but rather than trying to make me feel better, her words make it worse.

"Don't believe me?" she asks. Her voice is rough. "Let's go by his house. I bet he's there. I bet he and Deshaun are laughing at us right now."

Once more, I look to Caroline. *Why not?* I try to emote with a shrug. She nods and we turn at the next corner, heading to Deshaun's and Kyle's.

"But the clown—" I say, because I refuse to believe any of this. I refuse to believe Deshaun actually left her on the hilltop. He isn't that sort of person. He's a good guy.

Just like you thought Kyle was a good guy? I think, remembering how angry he became.

"Kyle was right," April says. "*I* haven't seen the clown."

"But you saw Deshaun disappear!"

She sniffs and wipes her eyes. "I don't know what I saw anymore."

I groan in frustration. "Well, look," I say. "*I* know what I saw. And I believe Caroline saw what she saw—there's no way she just scratched herself, and we *all* saw those shovels disappear. You have the wounds to prove they were there! Kids are missing and the clown is getting stronger and the more we fight among ourselves, the stronger it gets, and the less chance we have of finding the missing kids and the less chance we have of winning."

April just sighs in response.

I can't believe her. She *has* to know that was the clown on the phone. If it could conjure our worst fears—if it could actually scratch Caroline and break the sculpture in her house—it could easily mimic Kyle's and Deshaun's voices.

Are you so sure? whispers a little voice inside me. And despite myself, I start imagining all of my interactions with Kyle over the last few weeks. The short texts. The stilted conversations. The awkward half date at the carnival. He'd been growing distant. Haunted. Way before yesterday, way before the note and any talk of the clown.

It's just the clown getting to you, I try to convince myself. *You know Kyle loves you. You know this is just the clown.*

"There," April says. And even though there's pain in her voice, she sounds triumphant. "See?"

I shake my head and look up, pushing away the thoughts that had clouded my vision, and see we've stopped in front of Deshaun's and Kyle's house.

The porch light is on. Jack-o'-lanterns and fake ghosts and bats decorate the patio.

And the top right window—Deshaun's window— is lit.

I sit there, holding my breath.

Please don't be home. Please don't be home.

Then I see them. Both of them. Deshaun walks past the window with a football in his hands, laughing, and a moment later Kyle steps into view.

My breath catches.

Kyle catches the football Deshaun tosses to him, then throws it back.

Kyle pauses. Turns.

He looks out the window and looks at us in the street.

Sees me staring back, my heart breaking every second.

Then, with a wicked grin, he grabs the curtains and closes them, not breaking eye contact.

"Let's go," I grunt.

Caroline and April oblige.

I try to blink away Kyle's angry smile; it's far too easy to convince myself that the flash of blue in his eyes was from the streetlight or the moon.

It's far too easy to believe that he was home, safe and sound, with Deshaun. Laughing at us behind our backs. Saying horrible things about us behind our backs. Saying we'd made everything up. Saying we're just stupid children, the silly underclassmen, hopped up on sugar and imagination.

It's far too easy to believe that the three of us are on our own.

Kyle

"This is your fault," the clown—my father—says, his hands gripping my shoulders like vises. "All of this is your fault. You know that, don't you? Deep down. You know you don't deserve friends. And that's why this is happening to them. That's why they are slipping away."

I nod.

I can't help it. His words make too much sense.

"This is where you belong," he continues. "You know that too. This is who you are, Kyle. This is what you deserve."

Around us, snakes hiss from their open terrariums. Dozens. Hundreds. They spill over the tank edges, drape from the rafters, dangle from the single flickering light above me. The ground heaves and roils with scales and darting tongues.

I don't move. I can't move.

I've tried so hard to get away from here.

Tried so hard to convince myself that this was behind me. But how could it be behind me? This was a part of me. The only thing that wasn't true to myself was my friends. They didn't fit here. They weren't what I deserved.

"I'll make you a deal," my dad says.

He steps in front of me, but weight still pushes down on my shoulders. I can't take my eyes off my father in the horrifying clown suit, his black-and-white makeup and blue eyes. But I can see, from the corner of my vision, the giant boa constrictor that drapes over my shoulders, heavy as a boulder, heavy as all the things I'm running from.

"Join me," Dad says. This close, his breath smells like stale cotton candy and rot. In his eyes, I see my friends, screaming in fear. "Stay here. Where you belong. Let me scare you. Forever. You deserve nothing less. Stay with me here, and I'll let your friends go."

The snakes hiss and writhe.

I know I should fight. I shouldn't let myself believe him.

But deep down, I know the truth: It hisses within me, the voice of a thousand snakes, the voice of my father, the voice of the clown.

This is what I deserve.

My friends never really liked me. They were just friendly because we had overcome the clown together. Well, guess what. We didn't actually overcome anything. Our friendship meant nothing.

I meant nothing.

The best thing I can do is disappear.

The boa around me tightens.

I nod.

My dad smiles. His face cracks, his mouth widens, fills with jagged teeth.

He reaches up.

Turns out the light.

In the darkness, all I can see are his burning eyes.

All I can hear is the hissing of the snakes.

Until, a moment later, the darkness overtakes everything.

Deshaun

I'm alone.

As light flickers around me, I realize with dread where I am.

A fun house.

The neon and fluorescent lights illuminate violently orange-and-green walls, the colors so garish my eyes hurt. Spirals spin where windows should be, and the floor is made of uneven planks that tilt and wobble when I adjust my weight.

How in the world did I get here? And how do I get out?

Behind me, someone laughs. It's not a normal laugh. It's one of those bone-chilling horror-movie cackles that makes goose bumps race over my arms and my bones lock in fear.

And it's getting closer.

I run.

Down the hall, toward the fuzzy red light that I hope is an exit.

With every step, the hall stretches impossibly longer. The ground beneath me rocks back and forth as I go over the planks. Lights flicker, and the shadows behind them grow darker.

The laughter gets louder.

I run faster. Breath burns in my lungs and I kick myself for not trying harder in gym class because even though I don't know what's behind me, I know I can't let it catch me.

"We're coming for you, Deshaun," the voice croons behind me. *"And when we catch you, we will make you one of our own."*

The red exit light ahead gets closer, but behind me, I can hear the creature or creatures that chase me. Can hear the scurry of their footsteps.

It sounds like there are hundreds behind me.

I glance back, briefly, to see shadows darting along the walls. When I look forward, the hall has changed, become a long, spinning tunnel painted like a spiral. Just looking at it makes my head twirl. The red light at the end beckons.

"Don't run, Deshaun. Join us. Join our family."

The red sign nears. I'm close. So close.

But so, too, are the monsters on my heels. I run through the tunnel, lurching as vertigo hits and the world spins. As *I* spin. I stumble along, trying to keep my balance, trying to make my way to the red light at the end that rotates as well, and I no longer know which way is up or down or if they even matter anymore. My stomach lurches into my throat.

I fall to my knees.

Look back.

The shadows are getting closer, scuttling on all sides of the tunnel as if gravity doesn't exist.

I scramble forward, not taking my eyes off the writhing, pulsing monsters behind me.

When my hands and knees hit solid, flat, unmoving concrete, I almost sigh in relief.

Until I look forward, and I realize the red light isn't an exit after all.

The monster in front of me is enormous, takes up the entire space of the hall, so large and twisted it takes a moment to realize it's not a single monster after all.

It's kids.

All my classmates, twined together like some giant living statue. Their eyes are all burning blue, save for the two in the middle, whose eyes blaze red. They form a giant, toadlike creature, with a gaping mouth of children holding knives and cutlery for teeth. A long tongue of waving arms curls within its hungry maw.

I turn, but there's nowhere to run.

The spiral hall behind me is filled with more of my classmates. They cling to the walls, their eyes blue, their arms and legs bent in strange, spiderlike ways as they scuttle around me.

"*You can't run from us, Deshaun,*" they hiss in unison. "*You're trapped in this maze forever, and soon, we'll make you one of us. We'll make you hunt your friends.*"

Hastily, I yank out one of my protective amulets and hold it in front of me.

I hoped it would cause them to hiss and back away, like vampires hiding from garlic. Instead, they laugh.

"*You think your toys can protect you? Can protect*

*any of you? All your hard work, all your planning . . .
how does it feel to know it was all in vain?"*

The beast in front of me roars.

I'm completely surrounded. Nowhere to run.

The kids in the tunnel scuttle to the sides, clearing a space for something farther on. A silhouette stepping out of a faintly illuminated fog. A shadow with blue eyes. It doesn't rotate with the tunnel. It floats forward, its arms stretched out to the sides, clawed fingers screeching horribly against the tunnel walls. I drop my amulet and press my hands to my ears, but the horrible noise pierces through my brain.

Something floats above one hand. A pale blue balloon. There's something on the back of the balloon, but I can't see what.

"There's no use running anymore, Deshaun," the clown says. "Although if you would like to keep running, you can. I have you here now, and I quite like chasing. It's fun. Aren't you having fun?"

I can't move. My feet are frozen to the floor. All I can do is watch the clown as it nears, as the balloon in its hand slowly twists around to face me.

"Your friends don't want you anymore," the clown says. "They never did. But I'll be your friend. We're all friends here. We can play together. Forever. Wouldn't you like that?"

The clown kneels down in front of me. Holds out the balloon.

My hand trembles.

"Take it," the clown says. "Take it, and we'll play."

My hand tries to reach up to take the balloon, moving of its own accord, as if the clown can control even that. I fight it back. My fingers shake as I try to keep control. *Don't take the balloon, don't take the balloon . . .*

"TAKE IT!" the clown roars, its face contorting in rage, becoming even more shadowed and monstrous.

My control slips.

My hand reaches up to take the balloon.

But the moment my fingers are inches from the string, the balloon completes its revolution and faces me.

On it is Kyle's face. Serpents writhe around him.

His eyes are wide, and his mouth is open in a scream.

Caroline

We walk the rest of the way home in silence.

I don't know what to say.

I don't know what to do.

I know in my heart that that wasn't Kyle and Deshaun up there. I know what I've seen. I know what the clown is doing. But that knowledge doesn't help when Andres is the only other one who believes what's happening, and even he is having a hard time keeping the clown's tricks from getting under his skin. I keep glancing over at April, who walks with tears in her eyes and her arms crossed over her chest. She stares out at the night with a dreadful sort of resolve.

She's already made up her mind.

Maybe she still believes the clown is back.

Maybe she believes Andres and me.

But I know, from that expression, that she also believes that Kyle and Deshaun are against us now, and that the three of us are on our own. A deep, dark part of me fears that she is correct.

As we cross over the now-empty streets, the houses dark and the yards filled with shadowed pumpkins and decorations, it's easy for me to believe that as well. It's just us left.

The moment I think it, shadows creep from the houses.

They spread over the lawns like oil, covering everything in darkness. Shadows twine around the street lamps, engulfing them, swallowing the light.

Until it's just the road in front of us.

I narrow my eyes and keep my breathing focused.

It's just the clown. It's just the clown.

The rest of the world isn't *actually* gone.

Even if it feels like it.

Somehow, I manage to make my way home; the moment we turn onto my street, the lights return, and there's my house, warm and glowing and safe.

When we walk up the driveway, my dad opens the door and steps out.

"Where are the rest of you?" he asks.

"Kyle and Deshaun went back to their house," I say quickly. "Something about not sleeping well on a sofa."

My dad frowns but quickly perks up again. "Well, their loss! I have some hot chocolate on the stove for you. It just needs to be heated up." He hesitates. "Just, um, ignore the mess in the kitchen. I could *not* find that rat for the life of me."

Andres and I share a look as we walk in. April walks sullenly behind us. She doesn't even linger in the kitchen while I warm up the hot cocoa; she heads straight downstairs. My dad goes to his room, and it's just Andres and me, standing in the kitchen, which—as Dad had warned—is a complete mess. The cupboards are all open and rooted through— even the ones way up top—and the counters are a mess of kitchen utensils and odds and ends. I note a few new mousetraps in the corners. Empty, of course. I'm sure they'll remain that way forever.

There's no way they could trap the clown's nightmare creatures.

"What are we going to do?" Andres asks when April is out of earshot. "We *know* that Kyle and Deshaun are in trouble. I mean, that wasn't them up there or on the phone, right?"

I can see from his eyes that he's worried, and I know he isn't so much worried that they've been taken but that they might not be. That it *might* have been them on the phone and in the bedroom.

"It's the clown," I say soothingly, and almost laugh because I don't know *why* that's supposed to make either of us feel better. "It feeds on our fears. All of our fears. It's getting smarter. It knows we aren't just scared of sharks and ghosts anymore."

Andres sighs and slouches against the counter.

"I wish it *was* still just sharks and ghosts. At least then I knew what was real and what wasn't."

I raise an eyebrow. "Did you?"

"Well, not all the time," he admits with a grin. The grin slips. "I'm worried about her."

"She just needs time. She's worried about everyone, that's all."

"But what are we going to *do*?" he asks.

"*We* are going to drink hot chocolate," I reply. I

ladle him a huge mug and hand it over, then pour one for myself and one for April. "And we're going to go downstairs and make a plan and that way, when the morning comes, we'll be ready and rested."

"Are you sure that's a good idea?" he asks. "What if Kyle or Deshaun need us now?"

"I have no doubt that they *do* need us now," I reply. "I don't want to wait around either, but what are we going to do? Right now, April is convinced she saw Kyle and Deshaun at home. That leaves you and me. What could we do? We don't know where the boys actually *are*. Even if we did, I don't think we'd be any help. None of us are thinking straight. We know the clown wants to scare us. So we have to believe that means it wants to keep us alive. It can't scare a dead kid." I feel horrible the moment I say it. I refuse to think that Kyle and Deshaun might be dead. No. They're alive. Somewhere. And we have to be smart if we're going to have any hope of finding them.

"If you say so," Andres says.

"I do," I reply. "We need to stick together. April will see sense after a good night's sleep. I know it.

We just have to wait a few more hours until morning. They'll be fine. I'm sure."

I swallow my fear, as well as the words that repeat in my head: *This is your fault. This is your fault. And if they actually* are *in danger, it's your fault if they get hurt.*

Andres

All we know is that the clown has taken seven people, and that most of them were last seen near the carnival. We know that last time, we had to face our fears to defeat the clown. And we know that until we are able to face it together, we don't stand a chance.

It's not much more than we knew from the beginning, but before we can get into any sort of productive planning, we pass out.

The next thing I know, Caroline's dad (okay, *Tim*) is knocking on the wall of the basement, a tray of donuts and coffee mugs in hand.

"Knock, knock," he says. "Sorry, didn't want

to wake you, but it's almost noon and I figured you wouldn't want to sleep the *whole* day away."

"Noon?" Caroline yelps, sitting upright. "That's so late."

"I know," Tim says, coming in and setting the donuts on the coffee table between us. "I was surprised. Figured you all were up late watching movies and eating too much candy. Sugar crash. So, here's a bit more sugar to get you up and running again."

"Thanks Mr.—*Tim*," I say. I grab for a donut while he heads upstairs.

When he's safely out of earshot, Caroline looks between April and me.

"Did you have any nightmares?" she asks.

I shake my head. April does as well. There are dark circles under her eyes that tell me she didn't sleep as well as Caroline and I did, though.

"Same," Caroline says. "It's . . . I don't know, it makes me nervous. Why wasn't it haunting us last night?"

I shrug. "Maybe it got bored?"

April glares at me.

"Do you have a better reason?" I ask her. I stuff

another donut in my mouth. I have a feeling I'm going to need a lot of sugar to get through today.

"No," April admits. "I also haven't gotten any texts from Deshaun. Or Kyle."

I check my phone. Caroline checks hers. Neither of us has any texts. Well, I have one from my mom wondering when I'll be home, and one from my brother Marco saying . . . nothing worth repeating aloud.

"I'm worried," April says. "It's too quiet. This feels too normal."

And yes, she's right, but that doesn't mean I like hearing it. I'd much rather we pretend the clown just left town and everything is okay now, but I know that's not the case.

"I've decided that you're right," April continues. She looks to both of us, then to her hands. She's removed the bandages we put on before she went to bed, and her hands seem to have mostly healed, but they still look painful. "I don't want to believe that was really Kyle and Deshaun on the phone. I . . . I know what I saw in the graveyard." She flexes her fingers. "I know what I *felt*. I'm not going to let the clown get to me like that. But that means that both of them are in trouble. Because we most *definitely* didn't see them in Deshaun's window. That had to have been the clown."

I flinch at the thought of the clown being in Deshaun's room. Of all of us, Deshaun took the most time to ensure his room would be safe—he put out crystals and used incense and bowls of salt and all sorts of things to keep bad energy and spirits away. If *that* hadn't been enough . . .

"Which means," April continues, "we need to find them. I want to go by their house today. I want to see if they came home at all last night. If not, we go back to the graveyard and the carnival and retrace our steps. There *has* to be a clue. There has to be a way to save the others. Maybe if the three of us go back and try to dig up the grave, we can get somewhere."

"Maybe we should text them first," I say.

"No," April says. "I don't want to let the clown know we're coming. I don't want it to know that we're onto its tricks."

Now that we're awake and talking about it, I want nothing more than to run out the door and find Kyle. I have to know he's all right. I have to know that he and Deshaun aren't taken.

In that moment, not even the donuts taste good.

I don't know what's going on.

I don't know if Kyle needs my help or if he truly does want to be rid of me.

Either way, I feel totally helpless.

"It will be okay," Caroline says, putting her hand on my arm. "We'll save them."

I look to her, and there's a resolve in her face that fills me with determination: She knows that they're in trouble, and she's convinced we have what it takes to help.

I have to hope she's right.

We don't linger. After we've each had a donut (or, in my case, three) and changed out of pajamas, we head out the door. Caroline's dad doesn't even ask where we're going. We head straight to Deshaun's.

And maybe it's my imagination, but . . .

"Does it seem awfully quiet to you?" I ask.

"I was thinking the same thing," April replies. Caroline just nods, her eyes focused on the road.

The empty road.

And okay, it's not like a ton of people walk in this town, but it's Saturday and the sky is sunny and clear and it's fairly warm, and there is no one out. Like, literally no one. It feels like a ghost town. What's stranger is that there aren't any cars driving around either.

Jack-o'-lanterns sit dark on porches and sidewalks, not a single one of them smashed. A few houses have trees covered in toilet paper out front, but that's it. Ghost decorations sway lazily in the breeze, and leaves scuttle over the sidewalks.

No one is out walking their dog.

No one is going for a casual weekend stroll.

No kids are building leaf piles and jumping in.

The street is completely silent. No cars in the distance, no kids practicing instruments for band, no music, no TV, no yelling or giggling.

No screaming.

Our town is completely silent, and it scares me half to death.

"Something's wrong," I say.

"We're nearly there," Caroline replies. Neither she nor April contradict me. They've both gone as silent and intense as the world outside.

When we get to Deshaun's house, none of us rush

up the front steps. We stand there, staring at the windows, waiting for some sign of movement or life.

Nothing.

The curtains are all closed.

"Let's go as a group," April says.

"Yeah," Caroline and I say in unison.

"But be ready to run at any time," I say.

Neither of them says that that's overreacting. Right now, it feels like an *under*reaction.

We nervously make our way to the house, huddling close together. Our feet creak on the wooden porch. It's honestly the only sound out here—even the birds are silent.

Maybe that sound was enough, or maybe someone was waiting, but the door opens right as April's finger hovers over the doorbell.

At first, I don't see anyone inside. The entryway is pitch-black, too dark for this time of day.

None of us move.

None of us dare step inside.

"You came to visit me," says a voice within.

Deshaun's voice. And Kyle's voice. In unison. But also not them at all.

I take a step back. April and Caroline huddle behind me.

Shadows shift.

And out from the darkness steps the clown.

I flinch back, into April and Caroline, as the clown steps forward. Its smile splits its face, and in each hand it holds a blue balloon.

One balloon with Kyle's face on it.

One with Deshaun's.

"*They* came to play with me too," says the clown. "In fact, I spent all night finding others to join. Won't that be fun?"

The clown grows as it speaks, fills the doorway, cracks the frame.

"You three hurt my feelings," it growls. "You locked me away when all I wanted was to have some fun. But I have waited. I have grown. You thought you knew fear before, but now, children, now you will *really* know what it's like to be afraid!"

Deshaun's house rattles and groans as the clown grows, snapping the doorframe and sending dust and splinters down. But that's not the only sound. Screaming. I hear screaming.

It takes a moment to realize it's coming from the balloons.

"Run!" I yell.

The three of us kick into gear. We turn and stumble down the porch as, behind us, Deshaun's house collapses in a roar of concrete and wood.

We run down the block, and when I turn and look back at the house . . . it's completely intact. The front door is closed.

The only sign of the clown is the two blue balloons, now tied to the banister. Even from here I can see my friends' faces.

"What was that?" April says.

I flip around to look at her.

"Did you see it? Did you see anything?" I ask.

"No," she replies. Her eyes are filled with tears. "The door opened, but I didn't see or hear anything, and then you just yelled at us to run."

"The clown," I say. "It was the clown. It said . . . it said it had taken Kyle and Deshaun. It said it was spending last night gathering more friends, but I don't know what it means."

"I think I do," Caroline says, her voice shaking.

I turn around, my blood growing cold from the fear in her voice.

Behind us, a line of our classmates stands in the street.

Big red smiles painted on their faces.
Black diamonds around their eyes.
Their eyes burning bright blue.

April

"Can you see *them*?" Andres asks.

"Yes," I whisper, my voice cracking. And I really, really wish I couldn't.

It's all our classmates. Lined up in a row like they're taking a school photo. They're in their Halloween costumes—pirates and ghosts and cats and angels. Except they're all wearing the twisted face paint of the clown.

As one, they step forward.

"Let's get out of here," Andres says.

"Where?" Caroline asks.

"Anywhere!" I reply.

We bolt ahead and turn down a side street.

I turn back as we round the corner. The kids don't chase us. Instead, their smiles widen and they all tilt their heads to the same side as we flee.

They're watching.

Waiting.

For what?

I don't have long to wonder.

In moments, the town breaks into chaos.

If the streets were silent before, in one fell swoop, they fill with people and noise.

As soon as we pass, adults run out of their houses, screaming, batting at unseen monstrosities. Kids run with them, howling in fear as they're chased out of their homes. They don't seem to know where they're running or what's going on—they jump out into the street, flood the sidewalks.

"What's going on?" I yell.

Both Caroline's and Andres's eyes are wide, their skin pale.

"Help me!" a woman behind us yells out. "They're everywhere!" Then she screams and runs off, swiping at the invisible monsters flying around her.

"We have to get out of here," Caroline says.

"But where do we go?" Andres says. "If the whole town's like this . . ."

She swallows. She doesn't have an answer.

"What about our families?" I ask. I suddenly imagine Freddy and Mom having lunch, only to be assaulted by terrible nightmares. It makes my heart clench. "What if they're like this too?"

"We can't help our families unless we defeat the clown," Andres says, trying to keep his voice calm and level. He sounds a lot like Deshaun. "It's the only way."

"But how?" I ask. We round another corner, and this time the chaos doesn't follow us.

It's almost like the clown is waiting for our next move.

"You saw the balloons," Andres says. "And you were right—we need all five of us to defeat this. The clown has Deshaun and Kyle. We have to rescue them."

"It was in Deshaun's house," I reply.

"Yes, but Deshaun wasn't," Andres says. He looks back at me. "Otherwise, the clown would have put him on display to scare us. Which means he's some-where else."

"Underground?" Caroline asks.

Immediately, I think of the graveyard, and the crypt below the tombstone. I swear the temperature drops twenty degrees.

"No," Andres says. "I don't think so. That was before. The clown's changed. It's grown up. Think: What are the places that scare us most? Not like in our past, but present us?"

"I thought Deshaun's would have been the grave-yard," I say. "But we didn't find him there. As for Kyle . . ."

"Kyle was terrified of his home," Andres answers for us. "He's spent his whole life trying to get away from there. I bet that's where the clown took him."

We all go silent at the thought. The one place Kyle had been running from his entire life. It makes me hate the clown even more, to think it's taken Deshaun and Kyle to the places they're scared of most.

"But what about Deshaun?" I press. "Can either of you think where he might be kept?"

No one answers for a while. Caroline looks at me.

"Kyle's place is right around the corner—maybe Deshaun is there too. We can start there, and if Deshaun's not with him, we can head back to the graveyard to search."

"It's a start," I say. I want to help Deshaun, but Kyle's house is closer. And Andres was right when he was trying to reassure me earlier—Deshaun was the most prepared of all of us. I have to believe he's still fighting. "Let's go."

Kyle

Andres

We're going too slow. Too freaking slow.

Whatever is happening to the town . . . it's following us. Always too far to touch us, but close enough to see. Preventing us from turning around. Preventing us from pretending things might be okay if we gave up.

Horrors I can't even name fill the streets at our backs. Horrors I don't want to name. There are rats and ghosts, demons and clowns, skeletons and zombies. All of them chasing after innocent people. Turning the whole town into a terrible nightmare.

And, no doubt, making the clown stronger in the process.

My hands tremble so badly I have to shove them in my pockets to keep my fear from showing. Behind us is a raucousness of screaming and shouts, and I want nothing more than to cover my eyes and ears and drown it all out. But I don't. I can only try to face forward, pretend that everything behind us is a distraction. I can only try not to be afraid, not to run away, because my fear will just feed the clown.

There's nothing we can do to help them. All we can do is try to defeat the clown, and hope that's enough.

Finally, *finally*, we make it to Kyle's house.

I don't know if it's the clown's doing, but the house seems even more nightmarish than I remember. It stretches up into the darkening sky, shadows seeping from the edges and out the black windows, as if every inch of the place is bruised. Stranger still, this part of the block is completely empty; no one runs screaming outside, even after we pass. No, the scariest thing is the house in front of us. But that is enough. Even without all the terrible memories attached to this place and the horrible things Kyle told me about his time here, the house itself *looks* like a nightmare incarnate.

"This feels so wrong," April whispers.

I nod.

It doesn't look like there's anyone inside Kyle's house. But I know he's in there. He has to be.

"Come on," I finally say.

The moment I step into his yard, I hear it.

Hissing.

I want to pretend it's the wind in the trees, but I know it isn't. It comes from the house. A low, menacing hiss that snakes its way through my senses, slithers around my spine. Calling me and repulsing me at the same time. I stare at the house, anger and fear building equally in my chest at what this place has done to Kyle. At what it's *doing* to him.

Caroline and April step up beside me.

"Let's do this," I say.

The girls nod, and together we walk up the creaking front stairs, the sound of snakes growing louder with every step. *I'm going to save you, I'm going to save you*, I think on repeat, visualizing Kyle's face. His smile. His hand in mine. I have to do this. I *want* to do this. Kyle may have been moody, he may have been distant, but I would fight for him no matter what.

And this time, I have Caroline and April at my side to help.

The door opens the moment we near. The hissing grows even louder.

Only shadows wait within.

The girls and I look at one another. I can tell neither of them wants to go in. I can't blame them. I don't want to either.

But Kyle is in there. I know it. I can *feel* it.

I take a step forward
    into the house
        and step *on* something most definitely
        alive.

The snake I stepped on hisses and coils back.

I yelp out as the shadows shift and I realize the floor is covered by hundreds of snakes. Thousands of them. All shapes and sizes and species. Instantly, snakes curl around my ankles, wrap up my calves. Others drop from the rafters, draping around my shoulders and forcing me to the ground.

As the door slams shut on my friends, locking me inside the house, the snakes engulf me, smother me.

Light flickers.

Fades.

And in the heavy, suffocating darkness, the last thing I see is two burning blue eyes, and a wicked smile.

Caroline

"Andres!" April screams, banging on the door. She grabs the handle, but it doesn't budge.

I rush over to the window and pound on the glass. Inside, I can't see anything but shifting shadows and serpentine shapes. No sign of Andres.

April starts kicking the door, and if the rest of the world wasn't in chaos I'd fully expect some well-intentioned neighbor to call the cops. But the cops aren't coming. No one is paying attention to anything but the horrors in their own yards.

I run down the porch steps and grab a brick from the flower beds. Then, before I can think twice, I throw it as hard as I can at the window—

—and have to duck out of the way as it bounces off. As if the window were made of rubber.

Worry burning in my chest, I grab the brick again and throw it harder this time. Only to have it bounce off once more.

April continues to yell and grapple the door at my side. But it isn't working.

"Maybe around back," I suggest. "Maybe there's a door around back."

She doesn't hear me. Or if she does, she ignores it. She doesn't move from the door, doesn't stop screaming Andres's name.

Never split up. Everyone knows that. But I also know that there's no way we're getting in through here, and with April screaming her head off, maybe the clown will be distracted. Maybe it will be focusing on keeping us out from here.

"I'll be right back," I say. She doesn't respond. I run down the front porch and around the house. The world gets colder with every footstep.

As I near the backyard, I realize this was a terrible, terrible mistake.

Because with every step, the sound I mistook for wind chimes grows louder.

Becomes more musical.

I round the corner, and it's not a backyard greeting me.

It's the entrance to the carnival. Flashing red and yellow and white lights, striped pavilions and game tents, rotating rides. Tilting organ music sends shivers down my spine, the sound somehow entrancing and terrifying, all at once.

And arching over the dirt path is the sign, with the clown's plastic head atop it, its eyes burning blue.

COME PLAY, CAROLINE

That's the last thing I want to do.

I take a step backward.

This isn't right.

This isn't real.

I have to get April. We have to help Andres.

But when I turn to run back to April, I'm faced with a brick wall. I look around frantically. The wall surrounds me.

The only way out is forward. Through the archway. Into the carnival.

Into the clutches of the clown.

April

It feels like I pound on the door to Kyle's house for hours. I yank on the handle and kick at the door and beat on the window until my already-scraped fists are bruised and aching, until my throat is burning from screaming.

Until it finally sinks in that no matter how much I fight, I'm not getting in.

The worst part is, I don't know what happened to Andres. I didn't see a thing. Just him standing there one moment, and then the next, he was gone, and the door slammed shut behind him. Exhausted and terrified, I turn around and slide down against the door, tears making the world waver.

I cry.

I can't help it.

And it's only after sobbing into my hands for a few minutes that I realize that—other than my own breathing—the world is silent. Deathly silent.

I sniff and wipe away the tears and look up.

I'm alone on the porch.

Vaguely, I remember Caroline saying she was going to check the back door. Why hasn't she returned yet?

Even though I don't think I have any more room inside me to feel more fear, a spike of panic hits me. I shove myself to standing and, on trembling legs, make my way around the side of the house.

I swear it gets colder with every step.

I swear even the leaves crunching beneath my feet are muted. I can't hear a thing. Just the pounding of my heart in my ears.

I turn the corner of Kyle's house and stare into the empty backyard.

Caroline is nowhere to be seen.

Just a few bleached lawn chairs and a locked shed that looks ready to fall over.

"Caroline!" I call out. I'm no longer self-conscious about the neighbors hearing. I know deep down that no one is coming. No one is going to rescue us. "Caroline, where are you?"

She doesn't answer.

No one does.

I traipse up to the back door and try it. It doesn't budge. And once more, when I slam my fist against the glass window, it feels like hitting concrete.

I'm so numb I don't even feel the pain.

They're gone.

All of them.

Deshaun and Kyle and Andres and Caroline.

Gone.

And I know deep down it's all my fault.

Wind rustles through the alleyway. It sounds like laughter.

"Why are you doing this?" I yell out. "Why did you take them? Why didn't you take me?"

The clown doesn't respond. No one does.

"Are you scared?" I yell out. "Are you scared of me? Is that why you're afraid to show your face?"

Silence.

My attempt at insulting the clown hasn't worked.

It knows that it has me. Right where it wants me.

Without friends.

Without a clue.

Without any hope at all.

I walk back to my house and it feels like I'm walking through a dream.

I don't know how long I stayed outside Kyle's, leaning against the back door, hoping the clown would come out and try to scare me—because then I could slip into the house. Then I could try to rescue Kyle and Andres.

Then I'd know what I was dealing with.

But the clown never showed. Neither did anyone else. No matter how many times I screamed their names or walked around the house. I didn't see a soul.

As I walk down the deserted streets to my home, I realize that Kyle's house isn't the only place that's deserted. No one is outside anymore. The hundreds of kids and adults running and screaming are nowhere to be seen. The army of clown classmates has vanished.

In their place are streets of empty candy wrappers and haphazardly parked cars and silence.

I'm alone.

A numb sort of dread fills me as I walk to my front door. The handle turns easily under my shaking fingers, and the familiar scent of home wafts out.

Only, the air inside is cold. Cold as a refrigerator. I step inside.

"Hello?" I call out. "Mom? Freddy?"

No answer.

No Freddy running around in his Halloween donut costume. No Mom chasing after him trying to pry stolen candy from his grasp. The lights are all off, and even though it's still midday, the whole house feels unusually dark.

I flip on a switch.

The lights don't turn on.

"Mom?" I call out, stepping deeper into the house. "Are you there?"

The front door slams shut behind me. I yelp and turn around, but there's no one there.

I know it wasn't just a draft.

I just wish I could see the monster following me.

"Freddy?" I call out. My voice wavers. No response.

I make my way into the living room. Everything is normal, from the throw pillows on the sofa to the stack of wooden blocks Freddy builds with in the corner. The dining room is also completely normal, as is the kitchen. I peer down into the basement, and when it's clear they aren't down there either, I quickly slam the door.

Once more, I'm hit with the image of them running around outside and screaming, fleeing from nightmares I can't even imagine. Fears I can't even see. Did they run out and not come back? If so, why is everything in here completely in order?

I know they aren't up there, but I make my way upstairs.

Mom's bedroom is empty, her bed made neatly.

Freddy's room is a mess, but he's nowhere to be seen.

It feels so absolutely silent. Like everyone in the world is gone.

And that, more than anything, is what makes me go to my room and flop down on my bed.

"I'm alone," I whisper, staring up at the ceiling.

The moment I say it, I feel the weight of it, the *truth*. I am completely alone.

I've watched my friends get taken, one by one,

and I've not been able to help them. I haven't even been able to *see* the monsters they were running from. My mom and Freddy are both gone, taken before I ever had a chance to save them. Not that I could have saved them. If I couldn't see the clown or the nightmares it produced, what good could I do? I was helpless.

I am useless.

I am alone.

I'm too worn-out to cry. All I can do is lie there and stare at the ceiling and relive the nightmare of the last few days. Blink, and I see Deshaun vanishing before my eyes in the graveyard. Blink, and I see Andres thrashing on the sofa and freaking out about spiders and quicksand. Blink, and I see Caroline, shaking as she admits facing her mother's ghost.

Kyle, his expression stormy as he denies ever seeing a thing.

The clown came for each of us. It showed us what we feared the most.

So why has it left me alone? Why haven't I seen anything?

Then it hits me.

My fear is of being helpless, of watching my

friends being taken and not being able to do anything about it.

My fear is of being alone. Of losing my friends.

We've been slowly separating ever since last year, and I've watched it all with a terrible fear in my stomach. Knowing that one day, we wouldn't talk to one another anymore. There wouldn't be a fight. There wouldn't be any real signal it was over. We'd just wake up one day and realize we hadn't spoken in weeks or months. We'd go to different colleges. We'd grow apart.

And the only real memory we'd have of our time together would be fighting the clown, and eventually even that would feel unreal.

Defeat claws at my insides.

The clown has sped up the process. It's taken them all away. It's split us apart so we couldn't fight it.

The clown has won.

Only . . .

I am alone now.

My family is gone and my friends were taken before my eyes. This is the end.

Or it should be the end.

But I'm still here. Still in my room. Still alive.

Still afraid, but still willing to fight.

A flicker of warmth flares in my chest. A resolve. A hope.

I'm going to keep fighting. I'm going to get my friends and family back.

Even if it's the last thing I do.

I force myself to sit up.

"I'm not giving up!" I yell out. "Do you hear me? I'm not letting you win. You've taken everyone I cared about, but I'm facing my fear. I'm not afraid of being alone. The only one who should be afraid is you!"

I don't know what I expect. The clown to leap from the shadows and wail in defeat? The house to tremble as the nightmare fades and my friends and family return?

Silence greets me for the longest time.

Maybe the clown didn't hear me. Maybe it isn't watching. Maybe it too has abandoned me.

But then, from the closet, I hear a noise.

The jingle of bells.

The clown's demonic giggle.

"Oh, April, it wasn't going to be *that* easy," the clown says. The closet door slowly creaks open as it speaks. Shadows leak out from within. "You're alone.

You're abandoned. Your friends hate you. In fact, they never liked you in the first place. You should give up now. But since you think you're ready to play, let's play."

The closet door shakes.

Shifts.

Transforms.

Becomes a striped archway in red and white and yellow.

Light flickers behind it as shapes blur in and out of focus.

Pipe organ music tumbles out.

I stand, trembling, and make my way to the closet. To the archway leading to somewhere else entirely.

I see the clown farther on. Its silhouette wavers as if underwater, but it is there. Its eyes burn blue, and it waves at me, the motion menacing.

I step through, toward the flashing and flickering lights of the carnival—toward what is most likely my doom.

My bedroom vanishes from sight.

Andres

Darkness surrounds me. I don't move. I don't even breathe.

I don't want to upset the snakes I hear hissing in the shadows, the snakes waiting to strike.

As I strain my ears and try my best not to move, as I wait for the inevitable sting of fangs on my ankles, or for the clown's taloned hands to slip around my neck, I start to realize the hissing doesn't sound like snakes. It's too constant.

Light slowly materializes, blinking into existence, and I realize I'm most definitely not in Kyle's house. Not unless his parents have a very strange interior decorating style.

The room I'm in is dark and dusty, with a concrete floor and bare pipes overhead. A few of the pipes emit loud streams of steam, which is what I'd mistaken for snakes hissing. But the only snakes in here are the brightly colored stuffed animals draped from the pipes and rafters, and the neon snake lights flashing all over the walls, and the silly rubber snakes littered on the floor. I push myself up to standing and look around.

I'm alone.

No real snakes anywhere. No clown anywhere. Just the strange, empty room and an open door against one wall. Distantly, over the hiss of steam, I hear music. Pipe organ music.

One of the neon lights is actually a sign, blinking green against the wall: FUN HOUSE.

Wait . . . am I back at the carnival?

Before I can wonder how in the world I was transported here, I see a flash of clothing through the door.

My heart leaps into my throat.

Kyle.

I know it's him.

"Kyle!" I yell out.

He doesn't answer, but I hear his feet running down the hall. I don't pause to think. I run after him.

I jump into the next room and stop in my tracks. This room is filled with ancient Egyptian artifacts—piles of pharaoh's gold and glittering scarabs, giant statues of cats and the god Anubis, torches of live flame. And a sarcophagus.

"K-Kyle?" I stammer.

I take a hesitant step forward. The door behind me slams shut, and I hear a lock slide into place. I don't need to turn around to know that I'm trapped.

There is no other door.

This is a fun house, I tell myself. *A carnival ride. Nothing in here is real. Just like the snakes, they're all tricks.*

I wish I could bring myself to really believe it.

Something creaks, and I freeze. Nothing else moves.

It's the sarcophagus lid. I know it.

I glance around the room. Kyle isn't anywhere. The exit isn't anywhere.

My gut drops as I realize where the exit must be hiding.

It's all just a ride, I tell myself again.

Then I take a hesitant step toward the sarcophagus.

Instantly, the scarab amulets around the room start coming to life. They clack their golden wings and blink their ruby eyes. They each grow a set of large golden pincers that drip green venom. It makes it much harder to think this is all just a silly ride. Especially when they start scuttling toward me.

I don't hesitate any longer. I run forward, toward the large golden sarcophagus, the beetles swarming behind me.

I nearly reach the sarcophagus when it opens, emitting a foul bellow of green mist.

From the fog steps a mummy, arms outstretched.

I can't stop the scream that rips from my lungs. I skid to a stop, but there's nowhere else to go. The scarabs swarm around me, only a foot away, their pincers clicking devilishly, and the mummy staggers in front of me, swathed in old linen wraps with blue eyes glowing in its sallow skull, my name echoing from its mouth.

"Andreeesssss," it wheezes.

I have to get out of here. Have to—

"Ouch!" I yell. Pain sears my ankle. I kick on reflex, and one of the scarabs flies forward, toward the mummy. It latches onto the mummy's head and squirms around its eyes, momentarily causing the mummy to lose focus. I dodge past it, leaping over the scarabs with their venomous talons, and head straight into the shadows of the sarcophagus. I hope against hope my instincts are correct.

Behind me, the sarcophagus lid slams shut, throwing me into complete darkness. I can hear the click of the scarabs as they scuttle across the golden surface, trying to get in, and the thrashing of the mummy, trying to find me.

Tentatively, I reach out my arms. My fingers brush against something soft and sticky, and I recoil in shock.

Spiderwebs.

But there's no wall beyond them.

I have to hope it's the way out.

In complete darkness, with one hand in front of my face to keep spiders from dropping into my eyes and the other held way out front, I make my way forward . . . through the veil of spiderwebs.

Something scuttles down the back of my neck. My skin prickles.

I don't bat the spider off. Even though I want to with every speck of my being.

I know there are worse things in front of me.

After a few steps, I don't encounter any more webs. Just empty space. I keep my hands raised, just in case.

"Hello?" I call out. Well, whisper.

Light flashes, so bright it blinds me.

I wince and squeeze my eyes shut as darkness closes back in.

In the afterglow of the flash, I see my surroundings.

A hallway.

My reflection staring back at me.

Another flash. I keep my eyes squinted partway open. Enough to see that, yes, I'm in a hall. A hall of mirrors. And above me, lights strobe slowly, illuminating my way forward.

Flash!

At the far end of the hall, I see a figure. Kyle. But by the next

Flash!

he is gone.

"Kyle!" I call out.

I walk toward him, faster this time. I try to keep my eyes straight ahead, toward the end of the hall of mirrors. But with every

Flash!

I catch my reflection from the corner of my eye.

I wish I wasn't seeing my reflection at all. Each reflection is worse than the last.

Flash!

In the reflection, I am underwater, surrounded by sharks.

Flash!

And I am surrounded by floating skulls.

Flash!

And there are graves in front of me.

I pause.

Flash!

In the reflection, I'm kneeling in front of the graves. My family's graves. Their names carved into the tombstones.

Sadness hits me like a punch to the gut, an emptiness I can't shake. Because now, in between flashes, the vision doesn't go away. I watch in horror as my reflection in the mirror places roses on my parents' graves. *Flash* and my reflection lays a stuffed bear on the grave of my youngest brother.

And I know then what will happen if we fail. The clown won't stop at haunting us. It will keep going. It will tear our families apart.

It will kill everyone we love.

Rather than filling me with courage, it fills me with fear. With a bone-deep sadness.

Because I know we are going to fail.

Flash!

And there is someone else in the reflection.

Kyle, standing right behind me.

Flash!

He is crouched at my back. Only it's not just reflection. I feel him there. The heat of him. His breath by my ear.

"This is what happens when you stand up to the clown," Kyle whispers.

Flash!

Kyle's eyes burn into mine. They burn blue.

"This is what happens when you fight. Give in, and maybe it will let your family live. Give in. You were never their favorite, anyway."

Flash!

His hands are on my neck.

"They won't miss you," he whispers. "They'd be happier without you."

Flash!

His hands tighten.

"We *all* would be happier without you."

Flash!

Only this time, it's not the strobe but stars flashing across my vision as Kyle strangles me.

I reach up in vain. Grab at his hands clenched around my neck.

"Kyle, *please*," I gasp.

Flash!

Kyle smiles as he chokes me. But in the reflection, he's no longer Kyle.

Flash!

He is his father, snakes around his shoulders.

Flash!

He is the clown, dark diamonds around his burning blue eyes.

Fear floods me.

I've lost him.

I've lost him.

There isn't another flash.

Only darkness.

Only darkness, as the world around me fades, along with my hope of rescuing the boy I love.

Kyle

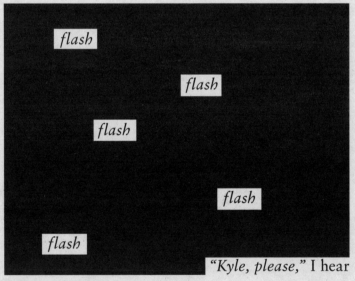

flash

flash

flash

flash

flash

"*Kyle, please,*" I hear in the darkness.

I blink.

Flashes of light.

I crouch behind Andres, my hands on his neck.

Why are my hands around his neck?

What am I doing?

In the reflection before us, I don't look like myself. I look like my father.

I look like the clown.

No. No.

I shake my head. Try to loosen my grip. Why am I doing this? Why?

"Give in," growls a voice in my ear. The clown's voice. *"Give in to who you are. Who you are meant to be. They never loved you. Never cared."*

"You're wrong," I whisper. I try to unclench my hands from Andres's neck. They won't move. Can't move. "I'm not like you," I say to my dad's reflection. "I never was."

Flash!

A thick white boa constrictor curls around me, tightening, squeezing. A boa with burning blue eyes. The clown stands behind us, watching, waiting.

I won't let you hurt him, I tell myself.

The boa tightens.

My grip tightens.

Memories flash: Andres and me at the park, laughing as we rock back and forth on the swings; Andres helping me move my things from my parents' house; Andres at the carnival, worrying we were growing apart.

Andres holding my hand, telling me he'd never abandon me.

The snake squeezes.

I force my hands to unclench. Darkness closes in, but I have to save him.

I won't let you hurt him.

I won't.

I won't—

April

My knees shake as I walk down the boulevard of the carnival. The air is thick with the scent of rot and popcorn, and the sky above is filled with clouds and churning red light. Music drifts around me, eerie and twisted.

The figure waving me in earlier is nowhere to be seen. But now I know where the rest of the town is hiding.

They're trapped on the rides.

My neighbors and classmates careen past me on a roller coaster that I know wasn't there the other night, screaming at the top of their lungs. Other adults howl in fear on the Tilt-A-Whirl, while a group of kids cry out from the spinning swings that endlessly twirl them over my head. And there, up ahead, are Mom and Freddy, strapped to the horses of the carousel. The horses go faster than they should, and their eyes burn blue; their teeth are wicked fangs. I run forward. But there's no way to reach them: The carousel is going far too fast to jump on, and when I run to the operating booth, I find the levers and buttons controlling it have been snapped off and graffitied with a clown's grisly face.

I run back to the carousel, any hope of finding Andres and Caroline immediately pushed from my head. Tears fill my eyes as I call out to my family. But maybe they don't hear me over the horrifying pipe organ music, or maybe they can't see me because it's going so fast.

Or maybe they're trapped in their minds, in the horrors the clown is creating for them.

No matter how much I yell and jump and wave, they don't look over. They stare straight ahead, eyes and mouths open wide in fear, screams silenced.

"Mom!" I yell out again. I drop to my knees in the dirt, staring up at the carousel as it spins out of control. "Freddy!"

"Don't cry," comes a voice behind me.

"You can join them," comes another voice.

"We can help," they—and others—say in unison.

The blood in my veins freezes as I turn my head . . .

. . . to see my classmates—those dressed in their Halloween costumes, their faces smeared with clown face paint—standing behind me.

"Yes, April," they say, their voices perfectly in sync. "Join us, and you can play with them forever."

As one, they take a step toward me. I leap to my feet.

There's a dozen or so of them, spread in a line. I don't know if I can make it past them, but I have to try. If I'm going to save anyone, I can't get caught here.

Their smiles all crack wider; their heads tilt to the side. As if they can read my thoughts. As if they know there's no way for me to escape.

There never was.

"You can try to run," they say. "But you won't save them. We're too powerful for you now. We have all the fears in your town to play with. And you, April. We will have the most fun tormenting you."

They take another step forward. Their eyes blaze brighter blue, and the air around them darkens with shadows.

As they step again, hands outstretched, I leap to the side and run.

I don't know where I'm going. I just know I have to get out of here as fast as I can.

The carnival is a blur around me as the clown classmates' feet thunder at my back, gaining on me with every second.

I race around a corner, and a terrifying sight faces me. The boulevard stretches far in front of me, way past the normal carnival boundaries. Rides and terrifying games border each side of the dirt road.

The dirt road that stretches up toward the hills, toward the graveyard.

Toward a house at the very top of the hill.

The hill that I know holds the clown's grave.

Even from here, I can see the house for what it is.

Kyle's house. Only larger, more desolate, with broken black windows and unhinged doors and a large neon sign in front that reads HOUSE OF HORRORS.

My gut twists.

For a moment, I consider turning back and going another way, but the clowns behind me are gaining fast and I know there's nowhere to hide.

Besides, I know if the clown is hiding my friends anywhere, it will be there.

I double my speed and run forward—

—only to be tackled from the side.

I cry out in shock as the kid barrels into me, but he doesn't knock me to the ground. Instead, he grabs my arm and propels me forward, toward the house.

It takes a second to realize who it is.

"Deshaun!" I cry out. Relief floods me. He's here! He's okay!

I want to hug him, but he doesn't slow down.

He grins at me, but he keeps his focus on the house up ahead.

"Did you really think I wasn't going to fight my way back to you?" he asks.

"But how—"

He shakes his head. "Later," he says. His eyes narrow as we race up the dirt pathway, toward the hills, toward the haunted house.

"First," he says, "we have to defeat the clown."

Caroline

I see them race past the booth. April and Deshaun.

Heading toward the last place I want to go.

And behind them, gaining with every second, are the clown kids.

If I don't do something, the kids will overtake April and Deshaun. If I don't do something, we'll all lose.

I glance around quickly. I've spent the last ten minutes hiding in one of the game booths—the dart game that Andres and Kyle had been playing the other night, only now, the balloons are filled with writhing snakes and bugs.

I need to make a distraction . . .

There, behind the counter, hidden behind teddy bears wrapped in plastic, is a megaphone.

I grab it without thinking and stand. Deshaun and April are only a couple of yards away from the base of the cemetery hill.

"HEY, CLOWNS!" I yell out, my voice amplified by the megaphone. "I'M OVER HERE! BET YOU CAN'T GET ME!" I jump and wave, and grab a dart from the counter and stab at the remaining balloons, creepy-crawlies flopping to the dirt, trying to make as much noise as I can. I worry it doesn't work.

But then, as one, the clown kids stop and turn to look at me. Their eyes burn bright blue.

They divert course and run straight toward me.

I drop the megaphone and run as well. I can only hope that Deshaun and April don't try to come back for me, otherwise this will all be in vain.

I dart through the stalls, knocking over pyramids of stuffed animals and pushing aside cotton candy stands and rusted popcorn carts and anything else that can slow the possessed children that chase at my heels. I kick over a trash can, spilling rats and garbage all over the street.

When I look forward again, I scream.

My mother's ghost floats in front of me.

She's more decayed than before, with chunks of her skin missing and her dress covered in dirt and mold. Worms crawl from her lips and the hollows of her cheeks, and the scent of her makes me want to throw up.

"You did this to me, Sunnybunny," she growls. "I'm dead because of you."

"No!" I yell out. Anger burns in my chest. Anger that the clown would throw this at me, anger that I almost let myself believe it. "She died because she was sick, not because of me. You are nothing, you hear me? Nothing!"

She howls in anger and lunges forward, but I leap to the side and run past her.

I don't look behind me to see if she follows. I don't care. I know it isn't her. Just the clown. All of this is just the clown.

I make a circle, running as fast as I can and trying to keep out of sight, grateful that I'd been in track, until I'm back at the boulevard leading to the house of horrors. Thankfully, Deshaun and April are far ahead, nearly to the door.

My relief is short-lived.

The clown kids stumble out of the game booths behind me. Even though I'm panting, they don't seem tired in the slightest.

I run.

Deshaun

Kyle's house looms in front of us. The graveyard is littered with tombstones and is as cold as winter. Up here, I can't hear the music from the carnival below, just the low, sad wail of the wind and the rustle of bare branches. The carnival itself stretches out to the foggy horizon, impossibly large. As far as I can see, there is nothing but blinking lights and terrifying rides.

The clown has taken over our entire town.

Soon, it will spread to the rest of the world.

"Do you think Caroline will be okay?" April asks nervously as she looks down at the carnival.

"I'm sure of it," I say. If only I could sound more

convinced. If only I truly believed that any of us will be okay.

We don't go up to the front door. We stand a few feet away, as if worried the house might reach out and pull us in, watching as Caroline runs up the hill, the clown children close behind.

I don't want to tell April about how I got here, about the horrors I saw and overcame in the haunted fun house. I will someday, but not now.

Caroline is fast—faster than me or April, for sure—and in no time at all she is here, her pursuers lagging farther down the hill. The clown children pause halfway up the hill while Caroline catches her breath beside us, April supporting her.

"Deshaun," Caroline says breathlessly. "You're back."

I nod grimly, reaching out to give her shoulder a quick squeeze. April isn't paying attention to the exchange. She isn't paying attention to either of us.

"They're giving up," April says.

The clown children stand there, watching us, smiles painted on their faces and their eyes all glowing demonic blue.

"No," I reply. "They've trapped us where they wanted us all along."

We watch as the clown kids disband. But they don't walk back down to the carnival. Instead, they spread out around the hill, forming a ring around us. Blocking any hope of escape.

Caroline and April and I look up at the house. To the flickering neon sign.

HOUSE OF HORRORS.

It always has been one. At least for Kyle. Now, I can only imagine the nightmare waiting for us.

The front door opens.

"We can do this," April says. "We're together."

I nod and squeeze her hand. "I'm not letting go," I reply.

She takes Caroline's hand, and together the three of us make our way up the creaking front porch and into the heart of the clown.

We're greeted with a long, shadowed hallway. Light comes from candles flickering with blue flame. The light dances on the walls, making everything move eerily.

We slowly make our way down the hall, pausing at shadows, flinching from the creepy dead objects on pedestals: skulls and mummified hands and taxidermy bats.

At least I hope they're dead.

Farther on, I notice windows along one wall, but as we get closer, we realize they aren't overlooking the town.

"Are those . . . ?" Caroline gasps in fear.

I stop short.

Five windows sit on one side of the hall, each revealing a room the size of a closet. And within each, cocooned in spiderwebs, are Jeremy and his brother Caleb, the redheaded twins Kerrie and Kevin, and pigtailed Eliza. They all float in space, suspended by thick wisps of thread, their eyes open and glassy, their mouths caught in silent screams.

"It looks like they're covered in spiderwebs," April whispers.

"No," I say, peering closer at the pink weave. "I think it's cotton candy."

"Are they dead?" Caroline asks. "Can we save them?"

April smacks her fist on the glass; the sound reverberates down the hall, making me shudder. *Well, the clown knows we're here now.*

But the wrapped-tight Jeremy doesn't move or

blink or register us in the slightest. He just floats there, suspended in cotton candy, staring into space.

"The clown is draining him," I whisper as things click. I look to the other kids—they're all just as pallid and gaunt as Jeremy. "All of them. It's feeding on their fears, just like it's feeding on the fears of everyone trapped in the carnival. I bet if we get these guys free, we'll have a better chance at defeating the clown."

"How do we get them out?" April asks.

I look around and grab one of the items from the nearest pedestal, a skull cast from solid metal.

"I don't think that's going to work . . ." Caroline says nervously, backing away a few steps.

"It has to," I reply.

I step back, shielding the others behind me, and toss the skull toward the glass with all my might.

It seems to fly in slow motion.

But it doesn't shatter the glass when it hits.

Instead, it disappears.

"What?" April asks.

I step forward, pressing my hand to the glass where the skull had—or should have—hit. The glass is solid. So what happened to the skull?

From down the hallway comes high-pitched laughter.

We all look over to see the clown prowling toward us, tossing the metal skull in the air as it walks.

"Naughty little children," the clown says. "Trying to break my home. Trying to steal away my friends."

It stops tossing the skull.

"But you'll be my friends too. You'll play with me. Forever and ever."

It tosses the skull toward us, and as it does so, the skull grows a body, becoming a towering skeleton that races toward us, its metal footsteps making the whole hall shake.

"Run!" I yell.

April and Caroline and I turn and run back down the hall. Only it's no longer the hall from before. Now other halls and doorways branch out around us, each of them with a sign on top: DANGER IN THE DEEP; HALL OF MONSTROUS MIRRORS; ENDLESS ELEVATOR; TUNNEL OF TORTURE.

None of those sound fun, but one seems less terrifying than the others.

"Come on," I say, squeezing April's and Caroline's hands as I lead them toward the hall of mirrors.

We run through the door, which immediately slams shut behind us. I fully expect the skeleton or the clown to knock the door down, but we're greeted with nothing but silence.

Silence, and pitch-black darkness.

Then there's a flash of light, and we shriek in shock as hundreds of reflections stare back at us.

The light strobes again, but this time when I look into the mirror, I'm not standing with April and Caroline at my side. Even though I can feel their hands in mine, I stare at myself surrounded by darkness.

Then another flash, and there are kids around me. Bullies from school. Laughing and calling me terrible names.

I squeeze my eyes shut and squeeze my hands, holding on to my friends for dear life.

This is all the clown's doing. None of this is real. None of this real.

"Come on," I say aloud. "We have to keep going. We have to find—"

"Kyle?" April asks.

Kyle

I skid to a stop at the sight of Deshaun, April, and Caroline in front of me. In front of us.

For a moment, I think it must be another trick. Another mirror. Another twisted reflection.

The mirrors have already tried that trick, many, many times.

But then Andres squeezes my hand and lets go and runs forward with a happy yelp, right into April's arms, and none of their eyes turn blue, none of them become walking nightmares or living dolls or any of the other terrible things we've seen in this maze of horrors.

"Andres!" April calls, squeezing him in tight.

And before I know what's happening, Deshaun is wrapping me in a hug so tight I can barely breathe.

His arms don't become boa constrictors. His jaw doesn't dislocate and try to devour me.

Instead, he jumps up and down, spinning me around, laughing so hard he might actually cry.

When he finally does step back, there are tears in his eyes.

"I didn't think I'd ever see you again," he whispers.

"Neither did I," I reply.

"What happened to you guys?" Caroline asks after prying April off Andres long enough to hug him.

My answer lodges in my throat. I look to Andres, who comes over and takes my hand.

"Kyle battled his inner demon and won," Andres says.

I take a deep breath. It's far too easy to remember how it felt to lose myself, far too easy to remember how it felt to have Andres's neck between my hands.

"It was the clown's own fault I won," I say. "It got me, for a while there. It had me thinking I was no better than my father. But that's what undid its power. It tried to make me turn on Andres. And he's, well . . ." I feel myself blush. "He's been one of the best things to happen in my life. Seeing him there reminded me of that. Reminded me that I'm not alone."

"And that you're loved," Andres says. He squeezes my hand tight.

"Aww, we all love you!" April says. She runs over and nearly tackles me with a hug. Soon, Caroline and Deshaun and Andres are wrapped tight around me.

I know I'm not the only one crying.

"Well, isn't this sweet," comes a voice.

The clown's voice.

"Five best friends, together at last. But I think you forgot someone. You forgot ME."

The huddle around me unfolds. Still holding hands, we form a line and come face-to-face with the clown.

It towers above us, easily fifteen feet tall, as though it has been stretched like taffy. Its arms and legs are thin and tipped with clawed hands, like spider legs ending in talons. Its head is skeletal, smeared with black diamonds over its eyes and bloody red lipstick, its teeth jagged and cracked, sharklike. Around us, the hall is transformed into a circular room of mirrors. The floor and ceiling too are mirrored.

The clown is everywhere we look, reflected a thousand times.

What is more terrifying is that our own reflections are nowhere to be seen. After being subjected to all the terrible reflected versions of myself, the absence makes me fear the worst.

"Do you like my little amusement park?" the clown asks. Electric-green drool dribbles down its lips, hissing when it hits the mirrored floor. "I was getting so lonely. I wanted a place where all my new friends could play."

"They aren't your friends!" I shout. I don't know where the bravery comes from, but I take a step forward, anger burning in my throat. At what the clown had made me do. At what I *let* it make me believe. Never again. "None of us are. You're alone, clown. You're alone, and once we've finished with you, you'll be dead."

The clown's eyes dart to me, spearing me in place.

They look so much like my father's.

And the moment I think it, the clown starts to change. Becomes more human.

Becomes my father. Although a monstrously large version.

"That's rich, coming from you," my dad says. His voice burns in my mind. It takes all my concentration to prevent myself from believing it's really him. "You think I don't have any friends? Please. *You're* the one who nobody loves. You're a mistake, Kyle. You're a mistake, and everyone knows it. That's why they don't love you. That's why you should end them."

As he talks, I feel myself sinking. The sensation begins in my chest as my heart sucks down to my feet, as my lungs deflate, as my thoughts cloud and darken. And I feel it, the serpentine whisper of doubt that slithers through my spine, repeating everything my father says, confirming every terrible word.

Except . . .

I feel Andres's hand in mine. Just as I feel April beside me, and Deshaun beside her, and Caroline beside him. All five of us, connected. Together.

These are my friends.

It's not just a friendship of convenience. No. Banishing the clown may have brought us together and bonded us, but it also made us something no one could touch and nothing could change.

It made us family.

A spark fills me, a tingling warmth that lifts me out of the depression, out of the doubt.

The darkness subsides, and I'm back in the mirrored room, and the clown is still just the clown.

"Did you really think that would work again?" I ask. "You'll never turn me against my friends. Never."

Andres and April both squeeze my hands.

The clown just cackles.

"Well," it says, "I had to try. Perhaps now I'll just have to try harder."

"We aren't scared of you," Caroline says.

"Yeah," Deshaun pipes in. "We're onto your tricks. You can't scare us anymore."

And maybe it's my imagination, but I swear the clown shrinks.

"You're nothing," April says. "You thought you could scare us. You thought we'd fall for it again. But we're friends. We stick together. No matter what."

I know it's not my imagination this time. The clown *is* shrinking.

And when I look around, I see its reflections freaking out—they shake their heads, or scream silently, or shudder violently—and I know that this is working. This is *working*.

"No," the clown says. "No, stop."

We step forward as one.

"You're nothing," I reply.

The clown shrinks, faster and faster.

And now it's crying. One by one, the reflections wink out.

"Now who's the scared one?" Andres says. We take another step.

"We're together," April says. "You'll never separate us."

"We've defeated you once," Deshaun says. "And we'll do it again."

The clown is normal height.

We take another step, its wailing so loud it almost makes me feel bad. Almost.

"It's just you versus us now," I say. "Not even your reflections are here to save you."

And it's true: The room around us is completely dark. No reflections, no mirrors, just empty black space. The clown buries its face in its hands, wailing and sobbing wordlessly.

"You're through," April says.

We take another step forward.

But then I realize it's no longer sobbing.

The clown is laughing.

"Stupid, stupid children," it says through its laughter. It slowly lifts its head from its hands. The grin on its face slices it clean in two, and its eyes burn brighter than ever. "To believe that would work on me again.

"That only worked before because I needed you. Because I was lonely. But I've made new friends. Friends who don't fight back."

The clown spreads its hands wide.

From the darkness come Jeremy and his brother and his brother's friends. The five of them form a line in front of us. Their faces are smeared with paint, and cotton candy hangs from their bodies like spiderwebs. Like the clown's, their eyes burn blue.

We all take a step back.

"And that means, stupid children, I don't *need* to play with you anymore. In fact, I think I've grown bored of you. I think it's time to destroy my old toys, don't you?"

It stands tall. The flames in its eyes promise destruction.

"I hope you run fast," the clown says. "Because if they catch you, you're dead."

The clown flicks its wrists, a conductor gesturing to a choir.

As one, Jeremy and the others run forward.

Deshaun

There's nowhere to run.

The moment we turn, we come face-to-face with mirrored walls. They circle us, blocking us in. We slam our hands against the panes, hoping to find some exit, some clue, while we watch the other kids run toward us in reflection. But it's not just the kids running toward us now—their fears begin to manifest in the mirrored room. Skeletons crawl out from the shadows, rats scurry from the cracks, and bats swoop down from the rafters, while the floor wobbles with quicksand. In that quicksand, I see shark fins slicing impossibly through the floor.

Behind all the terrible nightmares, the clown cackles, rising up twenty feet high.

"What are we going to do?" April asks. "We're trapped!"

We cower against the mirrors, looking around, trying to find an exit. But there's nothing—the walls curve all around us, trapping us within, with the clown cackling in the center like this is all a one-ring circus and it's the ringmaster.

Jeremy and the others slow when they're a few feet from us. Monsters swarm around them. My heart beats so fast it feels like it's going to punch out of my ribs. Caroline squeezes my sweaty hand and April's grip trembles.

This is the end.

We're trapped with our former friends and all their fears.

And this time, they don't just want to scare us.

They want us dead.

The kids take a menacing step forward.

"I'm sorry I dragged you all into this," Kyle whispers.

"Shut up," I reply. "This isn't your fault."

"But if I hadn't given in to my fears . . ." he presses.

"We *all* gave in to our fears," April says. "You can't blame yourself. You shouldn't be ashamed for being scared."

"You guys are the best friends I could have asked for," Kyle says. "Thank you for always being there."

I squeeze his hand, but I refuse to believe this is the end.

I refuse to believe Jeremy and the others are past saving. Even as skeletons and bats and rats swarm behind them, as flames flicker in the mirrors. Even with the clown behind them, cackling in glee.

And then I see it.

The ropes.

So thin I barely notice them at first, not through the monsters rearing up in front of us.

But there they are—thin pink strands that stretch from the kids in front of us to the clown's fingertips.

"I have an idea," I call out. "I'm going to make a distraction. And when I do, I want you guys to sever those ropes. I think they're what's fueling the clown and keeping the kids under control."

"But—" April says.

"No time," I reply.

Before anyone can stop me, before I can think that this might be a horrible, horrible idea, I run, screaming at the top of my lungs, away from Jeremy and the mind-controlled kids. Away from my friends.

As one, the kids and their fears turn toward me, and I can only hope that I was right about this.

April

"What is he talking about?" Andres asks beside me as Deshaun runs, full speed, away from the kids.

But I know.

Because the clown wasn't thinking—I can't see the nightmares the clown most definitely summoned up, the nightmares blocking its weakness from view. All I can see are the pink threads connecting the kids to the clown.

For once, being left out was a good thing.

"Cover me," I say.

As the kids turn their attention to chasing after Deshaun, I run after them.

And, one by one, I snatch the threads stretching

from the back of their heads to the clown's clawed fingertips.

First, the girl with pigtails: The moment my hand latches onto the sticky pink thread, terrible images shoot through my mind. The girl—Eliza—cowering on her bed while spiders scurry around in the shadows, wrapping her in a tight web and scuttling across her arms and legs and lips.

Then the thread snaps, and when it does, she collapses to her knees. I don't have time to question if she's okay. I run toward the next boy, the redheaded twin Kevin.

When I grab his thread, I see him trapped in a closet, while outside, skeletons slam their bony fists on the wooden slats, and he watches between the cracks, terrified, waiting for someone to save him.

He falls to his knees too, but when he does, his sister, Kerrie, turns, her blue eyes widening as she realizes what I'm doing. She lets out a terrible howl—and I race around her, grabbing the cotton candy thread.

In her nightmare, she runs through a dark forest, fleeing from bats that swoop and swarm, the gnarled trees around her drooping with their heavy, winged bodies.

She falls to the ground, but now I'm discovered.

Jeremy's younger brother turns from Deshaun and starts to chase me.

I dart under his outstretched arms and grab his thread—

—and am in a pit, buried under a pile of scratching, heaving rats. They suffocate me, their tails poking into my nostrils, their tiny teeth biting my skin—

and he falls to his knees.

One more to go.

But wait, where's . . . ?

Arms clamp around me, binding me tight. I kick and scream and struggle, but Jeremy has me locked to his chest, his arms squeezing. Stars explode across my vision. In the distance, I see Andres and the others running toward me. But they're fading, fading . . .

My only thought before darkness closes in is the hope that, if I die, they'll still manage to escape.

Andres

"April!" I call out.

I watch in horror as her eyes flutter closed, as the mind-controlled Jeremy squeezes her tight, suffocating her. She gasps in fear. I don't think she inhales.

I try to run forward, try to help her, but the ground beneath all our feet has become quicksand. The more I try to move, the deeper I sink. Already it's up to my ankles, and Deshaun is up to his knees. The only bright side is that—with every thread severed—the other nightmares disappeared. The other kids are still crumpled on the ground, hopefully asleep and not hurt.

It's just us and Jeremy and his quicksand.

And, towering behind all of it like a monstrous puppeteer, the clown. It glares down at us, angered at Deshaun's quick thinking. But it wasn't quick enough.

"I'm done playing," Jeremy growls. His voice isn't his own—it vibrates with the clown's anger. I struggle. We all sink deeper. "This one has always been troublesome. I think I'll kill her first."

Jeremy squeezes harder. April calls out.

"No!" we all yell at the same time. Jeremy just laughs.

"This isn't you, Jeremy!" I call out. "Come on, I know you're in there. You can't let your fears overtake you. You're a good guy. You'd never do this."

"That won't work," Jeremy replies with the clown's voice. But I catch it—the slight fear, the slight twitch in Jeremy's face when he heard my voice.

"Yes, it will," I continue. "I know Jeremy. He's a good guy, and he'd never hurt anyone. He's my friend. He knows we're here for him."

"You don't know his fear," the clown says.

It's *from* the clown's lips this time.

Before us, Jeremy still holds April tight. But the blue blaze in his eyes is dimming.

"That's not important," I say. "Everyone's afraid

of something. Those fears don't define who we are. What matters is how we face them. And I *know* Jeremy. He's strong. He'll never stop fighting. And he'll never lose to a monster like you!"

The clown howls with rage, and not just at my statement.

Jeremy's arms twitch.

Loosen.

April collapses to the ground in front of him.

Jeremy reaches up behind himself and grabs the thread on the back of his head.

It snaps.

The blue in his eyes blinks out, and he falls to the ground.

As the clown yells out, the quicksand around us disappears. We stand on solid ground. The moment I can, I run forward, toward April, the others at my side.

Caroline

She's breathing.

Thank goodness, April is still breathing. We gather around her, kneeling at her side. Jeremy is unconscious on the ground, but April's eyes flutter open the moment we near.

"What happened?" April asks.

She pushes herself to sitting, and I help her the rest of the way.

"It's okay," I whisper. "You're okay. Come on."

Deshaun loops her arm around his neck and helps her stand.

Because this isn't over. Not by a long shot.

The clown is no longer howling, but it still towers

above us. Its eyes burn, but the light is frantic. It looks like a cornered dog. I know that's when dogs are at their most dangerous.

"You horrible children," the clown growls. "I'll make all of you pay. I'll make each of you suffer."

"No," I call out. "We've already suffered. And you know what? We're still here. We're still fighting. We'll *always* fight. You know why? Because we have friends in our life. We have love. And you? All you have is fear."

"But fear is what makes you," the clown growls. "Fear is the worst thing in the world. You should be ashamed of your fear. You should feel *horrible*."

"No," Kyle says. "Fear is just an emotion. But it only hurts if we face it alone. We have each other. You can't hurt us. You're nothing. Because every time we face our fear, we become stronger. You thought that meant you could make stronger fears, but you were wrong. The stronger we become, the less room we have for fear."

"Yeah," I say. "You wanted me to feel like my mother's death was my fault. You wanted me to feel ashamed of that fear. But I'm not ashamed—I loved my mother, and I know her death wasn't my doing. You won't shame us anymore for being afraid."

The clown begins to shrink. This time, though, I know it's no trick. The clown's eyes are wide.

"You wanted me to fear that my friends were moving on without me," April gasps. "But even though friendships change, the love between us remains, no matter how far apart we are."

"You wanted me to feel helpless," Deshaun says. "But I know I don't always have to have the answers. Sometimes, just existing in someone's life is help enough."

"You wanted me to think Kyle didn't like me," Andres says, taking Kyle's hand. "But you've only proven the lengths we'll go to for each other."

"And you," Kyle growls. He steps forward until he's only a few feet from the clown, just within reach. But he doesn't seem afraid. Even as the clown shifts and twists. Even as the clown becomes the perfect image of his father. "You wanted me to think I was like my father. You wanted me to believe every horrible thing he ever said to me. But I know better. I'm a good person. And unlike you, I have friends. Unlike you, I deserve love."

"But, Kyle—" the clown begins.

Kyle cuts him off. "No," he says. "I'm tired of

your lies. You are nothing, you hear me? All you have in your life is fear. And that fear can't touch us. Not anymore."

And he turns his back on the clown.

The clown growls angrily. The image of Kyle's dad disappears, replaced with a horrible version of the clown—razor-sharp claws and long needle teeth, burning eyes and a snakelike tongue. It lashes out, scratches toward Kyle's back, and I have just enough time to scream—

Kyle

I feel it.

The gust of air.

But the clown's claw doesn't connect.

I watch it in the mirror in front of me. Watch as the clown rages and tries to slash at me.

But it can't hurt me. It can't touch me. Ever again.

I've done more than faced my fear—I've admitted my deepest shame: that my father *had* hurt me, that he *had* made me believe I wasn't worth love or friendship, that I was just like him. But in admitting that, in still having the love of my friends, I've made myself untouchable by fear.

No matter how hard the clown tries, no matter

how long its fangs or talons, it can't leave a scratch.

I don't have to say anything. One by one, my friends turn around. Turn their backs on the clown. Turn their backs on fear.

The effect on the clown is instantaneous.

It wails, flicking between shapes, trying to find something—anything—to scare us. It becomes a zombie, a demon, a giant spider, an enormous blue snake. We watch it in the mirror, holding hands, as it becomes more and more terrifying, as it plays to all our fears and more.

But none of us turn around. None of us cower. None of us let fear, or shame over having fear, take us over again.

It summons other fears. Bats swarm around it, mummies rise from the ground, snakes and rats and centipedes writhe at its feet.

Still, we stay strong.

It's okay to feel afraid now and again, I tell myself. *That fear doesn't define who you are. Love does.*

I squeeze Andres's and April's hands. I let myself smile. Showing them that I care. That I'm here. And that I know they're here for me too.

"It must be terrible," I tell the clown's reflection,

"to only have fear in your heart. You think you were scaring us, that it made you powerful, but we know the truth. You're scared yourself. You filled your life with fear. And that made you afraid. More afraid than we'll ever be. Our fear doesn't define us, but that's because we have love. We've faced our fear and shame. But you can't do that. All you have is fear. I feel sorry for you, clown. I don't think I've ever met someone so afraid."

Something happens then.

The clown stops flickering between shapes. Stops summoning monstrous nightmares. Though the nightmares don't fade, even as the clown changes.

The clown becomes the clown again—the original clown, the one that haunted our lives two years ago.

Only this time, the clown is the one that is afraid.

"No," it says. "No, you can't do this."

"We're not doing anything," I say. "You did this to yourself. And now, you have to face it."

"You're supposed to fear me!" the clown howls.

I laugh.

"Fear you? How can we fear you when you're scared of yourself?"

And in the reflection, the clown starts to back

away. Not from us, but from the horrible creatures it summoned.

The horrible nightmares that turn on their former master.

The clown howls in fear as it backs away from them. It turns and runs—only to slam into a mirror.

I *do* turn around then. The clown is no longer in the center of the room. And the room is no longer ringed with mirrors. Just shadowed darkness and a single mirror in front of us.

The mirror holding the clown.

I have an idea.

"Come on," I tell my friends. "Let's go. There's nothing to be scared of anymore."

"How?" Andres asks.

I reach down and take off my shoe. I look to Andres and wink.

"I may not be good at balloon darts, and I didn't win you that giraffe. But I'll win you this. It's the least I can do."

I chuck my shoe at the mirror.

Glass shatters. The mirror explodes outward, the shards shooting in all directions. But before it can hit us, it freezes. Pauses. In the shimmering pieces of glass I can see it—the clown, trapped in its own nightmare, terrorized by its own fears. Then the glass shoots back in, sucked in like an implosion.

Light flashes.

My ears fill with the sound of shattering glass.

I take Andres's hand once more.

I don't let go.

April

"What do you think?" I ask my friends after school. "Should we watch a scary movie tonight?"

Andres groans. "Who would have thought that *you* would become such a horror fan."

Kyle just chuckles.

I shrug. "Not much scares me anymore," I reply.

Deshaun rolls his eyes. "That's why I love you," he says, and kisses me on the cheek.

It's Friday. A week after we defeated the clown at its own game. A week after Kyle reinforced what I'd always hoped was true—and feared wasn't: that we were a team. A family. And we were always going to be there for each other.

We'd each gone back to our own families that night, and the story was the same each time. We got back to find our parents and siblings sound asleep in their beds. When they woke up the next morning, they didn't remember a thing. There wasn't even anything to remind them—the moment our vision cleared, we were back on the hill in the graveyard.

The clown's grave was no more.

The amusement park had vanished without a trace. Which just made me wonder if that too had been the clown's creation.

Even the streets had been cleared. No more haphazardly parked cars or signs of panic.

Life returned to normal.

Well, a new normal.

"You sure you don't want to have the sleepover at my house?" Caroline asks. "Dad's been begging me to have you guys over again. He feels bad about the whole rat thing."

Okay, so *most* signs of the clown had disappeared. Caroline's dad still remembered seeing the rat. But hey—maybe it *was* a real rat, after all.

"Nah," I say. "Let's go to my house. Mom already ordered pizzas."

"I'm in!" Andres says.

We start walking to my house, passing by Jeremy, who gives Andres a wave.

After the clown disappeared, Jeremy and his group had also woken up in their beds, unable to remember anything that happened. None of us tried to remind them.

"What do you think happened to the clown?" Deshaun asks.

"Dunno," Kyle replies. "I think it just ... vanished."

"It doesn't matter," I say. "It can't hurt us anymore. Not while we're together."

"And we'll always *be* together," Deshaun says. "Even as we get older and things change. We'll always be there for each other."

I nod, hope and love filling my chest.

As we make our way to my house, I know deep down that soon Kyle and Deshaun will graduate. We'll go to different colleges in different states. Our lives and our relationships will change.

Once, that would have scared me. But now, all I can feel is optimism.

Change isn't scary. Fear isn't forever.

The clown is gone. Our town is safe.

And even though I know, at some point, I'll feel sadness or fear or pain again, I'm not scared of it, not like I was before.

Our friendship has seen us through sharks and ghosts and killer clowns. It can last through anything, even something as mundane as college.

"Hey, look," Kyle says. He pauses and reaches down into the grass.

And picks up a tiny garter snake.

"No way," Andres says.

Kyle holds the snake up to his face. The thing is the size of an earthworm.

"I can't believe I ever let these scare me," Kyle says. Then he chuckles. "But I also can't see why my dad was obsessed with them. I think he thought they were scary. But they aren't, are they?" He holds it out to Deshaun. "Kinda cute, huh? Think your parents would let us keep him?"

"Not in a million years," Deshaun says with a laugh.

Kyle smiles and gently places the snake back in the grass. We keep walking.

Toward my house. Toward another night of bad movies and great junk food. I know we don't have many of those nights left.

Everything changes.

And for once, I'm actually pretty excited about it.

Acknowledgments

It's rare for me to remember the precise place a book was born, but this one was created on a bus in Iceland, heading toward the airport and a new phase of life. And all the fears that go along with big changes. So my first and dearest thanks goes to Jana Haussmann, for all her support, and for her well-timed news on that Icelandic bus that *The Fear Zone 2* was going to be brought into the world. I owe so much to her and the entire Scholastic Book Fairs team—their hard work and passion for these books has changed my life.

My deep thanks, too, to David Levithan, editor-extraordinaire, for continually pushing me and these books to be their best versions. One day, you won't have to remind me how much I overuse pet phrases—what a blood-chilling notion.

My thanks as well to my colleague and friend Will Taylor, for always providing a keen eye. And my family, for their continued love and support no matter where my path leads.

And finally, my thanks to you, dear readers, for joining me on this zany ride. The world can be a scary place, but hopefully, through these books, you've found some humor, some thrills, and the strength to face what comes.

About the Author

K. R. Alexander is the pseudonym for author Alex R. Kahler.

As K. R., he writes creepy middle grade books for brave young readers. As Alex—his actual first name—he writes fantasy novels for adults and teens. In both cases, he loves writing fiction drawn from true life experiences. (But this book can't be real . . . can it?) Alex has traveled the world collecting strange and fascinating tales, from the misty moors of Scotland to the humid jungles of Hawaii. He is always on the move, as he believes there is much more to life than what meets the eye.

You can learn more about his travels and books, including *The Collector, The Collected, The Undrowned, The Fear Zone,* and the books in the Scare Me series, on his website curtedlibrary.com. He looks forward to scaring you again . . . soon.

Keep reading for more scares from K. R. Alexander!

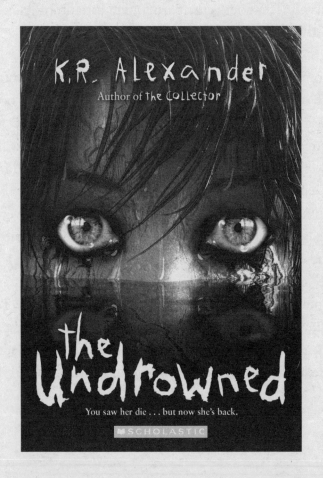

1

Wednesday is *not* going my way, and I know just who is going to pay for it.

I still have my parents' argument ringing in my ears when I get to school. All morning they've been fighting. Not just about each other and how they both *work too much*, which is what they usually spend breakfast fighting about, but because I failed a spelling test.

One stupid spelling test.

Now they're refusing to take me on a day trip to Rocky River Adventure Park this Saturday like they promised, all because I misspelled a few words like *possessed* and *allegory*. (Who needs to know how to spell those, anyway? I always have my phone, and that can fix spelling for me. As if I'd ever even use any of the spelling words in the first place.)

So, no theme park for me. My so-called friends will still be going, because *their* parents aren't jerks like mine. And I'm sure I'll hear all about how amazing it was on Monday.

All I get to look forward to is a weekend of doing homework while my parents continue to argue downstairs and my sister plays video games with her friends, and none of it's fair because it's not really my fault that I didn't have time to study for the spelling test. I'd been too busy writing the essay that Rachel was supposed to do for me. She let me down. Again.

It's her fault.

All of this is her fault.

And I'm going to make sure it's the last time.

I stomp through the school's front doors and down the hallway, and it must be pretty clear that I'm angry—kids actually step away from me, parting and going quiet so I can pass, hoping they won't be the latest victims of my wrath. I shove past a few of them. Knock books out of a nerd's hands, slam another kid into his friend. No different from my normal entrance.

But the truth is, I barely even see them. They're not worth my time, let alone my anger.

Rachel is.

I see her at her locker before she ever sees me. Short and pretty, with long black hair and perfect skin and big blue eyes. I'm tall and have the same black hair, but my skin is far from perfect, which some kids used to make fun of me for, until I started pushing back and proving I wasn't someone you could make fun of. Now the only bully in this school is *me*.

"You," I growl when I reach her locker. I slam it shut to emphasize my point.

She jumps back with a yelp and clutches her sketchbook to her chest with both hands, eyes wide and lip already quivering like a baby's. She knows when I'm in a bad mood, and it's clear she knows this is worse than all the rest.

"I—"

"Shut up," I say. "Do you have any idea what you've done?"

"I—I—" she stutters.

"Because of you and your stupid little pea-brain,

my parents aren't taking me to the adventure park this weekend. You were supposed to write my essay, but you didn't, and because of that I couldn't study for the spelling test. It's your fault I failed. And you're going to pay for it."

I want to shove her against the locker, but I hold myself back. Partly because I know she'd just start crying and partly because I see our principal, Mr. Detmer, out of the corner of my eye. He's watching us. I don't need to get detention again—the last thing I need is to be grounded.

I lower my voice.

"I'm going to get you back for this." I look into her eyes, and she looks to her feet. "If I have to suffer, so will you. Now, hand it over."

She nods. She doesn't ask what I want or what I mean. She already knows.

We have this down to an art. Almost a symbiotic relationship—a situation where both parties benefit from the other's skills. I learned that term in science.

In this case, it means I don't beat her up, and she does my homework and pays for my lunch.

It wasn't always like this with us.

We used to be friends. Best friends.

Used to.

I can't even really imagine it anymore. I guess we were friends when we were both younger. Weaker.

Now I'm no longer weak; she taught me that friendship is the ultimate weakness. Friends can hurt you. Friends can make your whole life miserable if they know everything about you. And from her betrayal, I grew strong. I used that lesson against her, because she deserved all that and more.

Am I using her?

Sure.

But it's the only use she has in our school. Otherwise, she's nothing. I make sure of it.

She opens her locker again—which takes a second, since she has to reenter her code—and pulls out a folder. I flip it open and check, but she hasn't disappointed me on this, at least. She knows not to let me down again. The social studies homework we got yesterday is done, along with the math practice sheets. And there, in the front pocket, is the five dollars she gives me every day for lunch.

I've never asked where she gets the money.

Probably her parents. They're loaded. They even have a pool in their backyard. Perfect Rachel and her perfect life. Her perfectly useless life.

She could give me a million dollars, and she'd still owe me.

I snap the folder shut and slam her locker closed again.

I miss her fingers. Barely.

Gotta keep her a little scared. Tears well in her eyes.

I don't say anything when I turn and stomp down the hall to my locker. I shove into another kid on the way, making her drop her bag, her books and homework scattering all over the floor. Mr. Detmer calls out to me, but I'm already around the corner, and I know he won't follow.

He's a little scared of me, too.

He should be.

They all should be.